Keep Smiling Through

ANN RINALDI

Keep Smiling Through

Harcourt Brace & Company

SAN DIEGO   NEW YORK   LONDON

Requests for permission to make copies of
any part of the work should be mailed to: Permissions Department,
Harcourt Brace & Company, 6277 Sea Harbor Drive,
Orlando, Florida 32887-6777.

This is work of fiction. Any resemblance to any actual place or
person, living or dead, is unintended.

Library of Congress Cataloging-in-Publication Data
Rinaldi, Ann.
Keep smiling through /Ann Rinaldi.
p.   cm.
Summary: A ten-year-old girl living in
middle-class America during World War II learns the painful
lesson that doing what's right is not
always an easy thing to do.
ISBN 0-15-200768-7
ISBN 0-15-201072-6 (pbk.)
1. World War, 1939–1945—United States—
Juvenile Fiction. 2. German Americans—Juvenile Fiction.
[1. World War, 1939–1945—United States—Fiction.
2. German Americans—Fiction. 3. Courage—
Fiction. 4. Stepmothers—Fiction.] I. Title.
PZ7.R459Ke 1996
[Fic]—dc20   95-31214

The text was set in Berkley Old Style Book.
Designed by Lori J. McThomas
First edition
A B C D E
A B C D E (pbk.)
Printed in Hong Kong

To all who served abroad to make the world free,
and to all who kept smiling through
on the home front.

ACKNOWLEDGMENTS

I am indebted to Susan Feibush, Librarian at the Somerset County Library in Bridgewater, New Jersey, for helping me run down facts on the Bund meetings in this state during the war. Susan was tireless in her efforts.

Thanks go to Karen Grove, my editor at Harcourt Brace, for her ability to see the merits of the story I submitted. And to the students of Edgewood Elementary School in Yardley, Pennsylvania, whose eyes went wide when I told them what it was like to be a child in this country during World War II. Their interest spurred me to write this book in the first place.

AUTHOR'S NOTE

This is a work of fiction. All the people and events portrayed in the book are the products of my imagination or are included to lend authenticity to the story.

World War II was the background music against which my childhood was played out. I was seven years old when war broke out. I do not remember what the world was like before it and, once it started, I thought the atmosphere of war was normal.

I clearly understood what was going on, of course. Everybody did. We were fighting to destroy a monstrous evil that threatened to take over the world. We had to win. In order to do this everybody had to sacrifice and pull together. So we did just that.

Fear was all around. Nobody bothered to shield children from it. On Saturday afternoons at the movies we may have watched films dedicated to fantasy and frivolity, but the newsreels gave us the larger-than-life black-and-white images of London being bombed, refugees fleeing their homelands, our ships being torpedoed in high seas, our men fighting in the trenches, on the beaches, and in the air, and in general, all the turmoil, confusion, destruction, cruelty, and terror that accompanies a war. Then on to a Donald Duck cartoon or *Lassie Come Home*.

We children on the home front were expected to integrate all the horrific images of war into our lives and not only adjust, but do our chores and schoolwork, save our pennies and buy war stamps, and give up such things as sugar, extra shoes, and all hope of new toys—and keep our mouths shut and stay in the background, too, while the grown-ups around us went about the grim business of survival in a world gone mad.

Today, my six-year-old grandson can get his mother to send away for a policeman's outfit from a catalog. It will come with everything a policeman uses, everything except a gun—because today's parents think that if their children don't see a toy gun or know that a policeman uses one, they will become better people.

Perhaps they are right. The jury is still out on that one. My generation stakes no claim to perfection. And each generation works with the legacy it is given. Ours was war.

In my childhood, bombsights came in cereal boxes. With instructions. Most of our radio programs involved war and killing the enemy. We went about our business of killing Germans and "Japs" on the playground. Nobody had the least bit of concern. Where today's kids know what product is the latest commercial tie-in to a new book or movie, I knew the difference between a P-38 and a P-41. I knew all about Flying Fortresses. I knew what the *Luftwaffe* was (the German air force) and who the Desert Fox was (German Field Marshal Erwin Rommel).

I did not have a favorite rock star, but a favorite general (Douglas MacArthur). I knew about places like Guam, the Marianas, Leyte Gulf, the Battle of Midway.

I knew all the excitement and the theater of war, and the bleak realities. I absorbed them as I absorbed the fact of gold-starred flags in the window when a family member was killed in action and gas ration stickers on the car.

Life became deprived and threadbare

during the war, but it also became incredibly rich in commodities like pride and accomplishment.

And for all of it, as a generation of youngsters we did not grow up hating, vicious, fearful, or dysfunctional. Though today, I still cannot look at a movie involving Nazis, for all the old images and fears that it invokes. And whenever I hear sirens I think of air raids.

Most of the kids I grew up with became whole, contributing citizens, stayed married to their original mates, raised good children, worked hard, and took their lumps as they came, without complaining. Most are happy. Why? I think it is because we learned, early on, the distinct difference between good and evil. And what was important. It is that simple.

Also we learned one other thing. There is something called the "common good." As children we were taught to sacrifice for it. We were taught that our own needs and desires were not that important. As for our troubles, well, somebody always had it worse. If you got potato soup for supper because meat was rationed, you were lucky. The children in Europe were starving. Others suffered in concentration camps. How lucky to be an American!

I still think that way. It's simplistic, I know, and nowhere near politically correct these days. But my children somehow feel the same way. And if I have anything to say about it, so will my grandchildren.

As Winston Churchill, British statesman and one of the heroes of World War II, said, ". . . democracy is the worst form of Government except all those other forms that have been tried from time to time."

Ann Rinaldi
1 August 1995

Keep Smiling Through

CHAPTER

1

I was ten the year I learned that you can be good and do the right thing and sometimes it all goes bad for you anyway.

It isn't a useless thing to know. I just wish I hadn't learned it so soon, that I could have gone on forever believing what our radio heroes were teaching us in that spring of 1944: that all you have to do is stand up for truth and have an unswerving sense of justice and you will be rewarded in the end.

It doesn't happen that way. And that was the one thing Queenie didn't tell me before she left us. She told me everything else, though, so I really can't blame her. If it wasn't for what she told me, I never would have made it through.

I don't blame her for leaving. Nothing she

did for us satisfied my father and Amazing Grace.

Amazing Grace is the name Queenie gave to my stepmother. It fits. She is amazing, but in a way I can't figure.

How can anybody be that ornery and live? Never mind. She married my father after my mother died. And since then she's killed happiness in our house wherever it tried to grow. That is her best talent. Queenie says everybody has one.

"Can you keep a secret, Kay?" Queenie asked as she put the last of the dried supper dishes away.

"Yes," I said. "Have I told anybody you're teaching me to tap-dance?"

"Ssh," she said. "Amazing Grace would kill you if she knew."

"I don't care."

"Yes, you do. You doan wanna get her in a rage."

"You're the best tap dancer, Queenie. I love you as much as I love Shirley Temple. But Amazing Grace says Shirley Temple is too old for me to love, that she's a teenager now, like my sisters."

Queenie laughed. "Shirley's more than a tap dancer. That's not her best talent."

"What is, then?"

"Bein' a little girl forever. For all little girls, everywhere. But now, 'nuf talk 'bout Shirley. I want to tell you a secret. I'm leavin' tonight."

"Leaving?" The word made no sense.

Oh, I *understood* the word, all right.

My mother had died when I was born. If that wasn't leaving, nothing was. But not Queenie. I could feel the world moving under my feet.

"You can't leave," I said. "You already *left* the South, where your people are poor and not treated right. This is where you *came*. Where would you go to from here?"

She laughed again. "New York," she said.

"But then you can come back at night!" My father went to work in New York every day and came back at night.

"No, honey, I can't. I'm goin' with my prince. He's comin' to get me tonight. Now, I told you he has a good job in the Brooklyn Navy Yard. And I told you I came to work for your father just to hold me over, until my prince could come get me."

I felt ready to cry. "I didn't think he would come, Queenie."

She sat on a chair and drew me toward her. "I told you, too, that princes *always* come. Sooner or later, if you wait long enough, all girls' princes come to get them. Like in the Walt Disney movies. If you believe. Didn't I tell you that?"

"Yes." I looked at her, into her yellow-brown eyes. Queenie is the only person I know who has less to believe in than I do. And yet she believes, more than anybody, in wishing on stars, in whistling while you work, in letting your conscience be your guide. And in princes.

"I'm glad your prince is coming, Queenie," I said. I wasn't glad, but it was the right thing to say. "But I don't know how I'm going to stand it here without you."

"You'll stand it, baby."

"How?"

"How?" She thought for a moment. Then she smiled. "You know that song that lady, Vera Lynn, sings on the radio? The one your sisters like? 'Bout smilin' through."

I nodded yes.

"You just keep thinkin' of that song. And keep smilin' through. And like it says, we'll meet again someday. Meanwhile, you'll grow up into somethin' fine."

"A tap dancer," I said. "I'll practice even if you're not here. And Mary said that this Saturday, when we go into town for my shoes, she'll get me Mary Janes."

Queenie sighed and shook her head sadly. "She oughtn't to do that, baby."

"Queenie, you know I want Mary Jane shoes more than anything in the world," I whispered.

"I know, Kay. But we doan always get what we want in life. Sometimes we get other things instead."

There was nothing I wanted more now than a pair of Mary Janes. "All the girls in school have them, Queenie."

"I know that, too," she said in that singsongy, patient way of hers, "but if Mary buys them, Amazing Grace will only make her take them back. She says they're bad for your feet."

"But if Mary buys them, maybe it will be okay. You know Mary is Amazing Grace's favorite."

"That woman doan have favorites. She doan like nobody. Not even herself. Besides, with the war on an' you only bein' allowed two pair of shoes a year, for certain Amazing Grace won't allow one to be Mary Janes. Now doan you make Mary buy them, or there will be trouble. An' I won't be here to hold you when your stepmother gets done with her lashin' out."

"Well, even if I don't get Mary Janes, I'll be a tap dancer," I said.

She touched my hand. "You know I never lie to you, baby."

My heart fell. No, she didn't.

"You may not be a tap dancer, Kay. But you'll be somethin' fine. Remember, Queenie told you so."

"How will I become something fine?" I asked.

She got up to fold the dish towels and hang them on the rack. "Doan know, baby. But you remember. The Lord doan close a door, but He opens a window. Jus' like He did for me. You just' keep smilin' through."

Queenie was almost as big on the Lord as she was on Walt Disney. I go to Catholic school, where Sister Brigitta smacks me with a ruler when I can't do my times tables. So I was having a little trouble believing the Lord was going to open any windows for me.

Besides, right now I wasn't so happy with the Lord. He had opened a window for Queenie. And now she was leaving.

———

Later that night, I lay in my bed listening. And when everybody else was asleep and the house was quiet, I heard Queenie creep down the attic stairs by my room. I got out of bed and knelt on the floor at my window. For a few minutes, I waited.

The night was bright, cold, and moon flooded. I heard the car's wheels on the gravel drive before I saw it. Then, when I did see it, I thought it looked just like a chariot should look. Long and shiny and low.

It stopped. Below me I saw Queenie come out of the house. Someone inside the car opened the door. And just before Queenie got in, she turned and looked up at my window and waved. I waved back. Then she got into the car, the door thudded closed, and the car moved slowly around the drive, out of my sight.

CHAPTER

2

The next morning my father stood at the foot of the attic stairs, yelling for Queenie. "Time to get up and start breakfast!"

But, of course, there was no Queenie. I dressed quickly and slipped downstairs. The kitchen was cold. No one had started the fire in the stove.

My sisters, Mary, who was sixteen, and Elizabeth, seventeen, knew they should do something, so they were scurrying around trying to get breakfast on the table. They both had early shifts at the arsenal, where they worked in the office. My father had to catch the 7:35 to New York. My brother Martin, who was fourteen, was putting wood in the kitchen stove. Tom, twelve, came in from outside with a fresh pail of milk from our one cow.

"Where is she?" my father asked about Queenie.

Nobody answered.

"Martin and Tom, get dressed for school," my father ordered. "Kay, go up and wake Queenie."

"She's gone," I said.

"Gone?" He looked at me as if the fault were mine. "Where?"

"I don't know," I lied. "But I heard a car outside last night and I looked out the window, and she drove away in the car."

"Why did she leave?" My father was bewildered. People left him all the time. Since my mother had died we'd had about ten housekeepers.

"I don't know, Daddy," Mary said, "but come and sit. I'll make your eggs, just the way you like them."

He sat at the dining-room table and Mary fussed around him. Elizabeth didn't. She ate her breakfast alone in the kitchen, then she started to make sandwiches for herself and the rest of us.

"Daddy," Mary said, "Beverly's father said Tony and Marie are looking for work." Beverly Vineland, who lived across the road, was Mary's best friend.

"Have Beverly send them over to see me

tonight, then. Girls, you'll have to do the dishes when you come home tonight. And see to supper. Kay, pile the dishes in the sink before you leave for school. Mary, keep some eggs warmed on the stove for your mother."

Amazing Grace was still sleeping. She was expecting a baby. Her first. And she needed lots of sleep, good food, and waiting on.

"Daddy, Kay doesn't have mittens and it's cold out," Mary told him.

He was finishing his breakfast. "Did you lose them again?" he asked sternly.

"I left them on the school bus," I said.

"Then ask everyone on the school bus if they found them."

There was no way I could do that. We rode five miles to St. Bridget's on the bus for the public-school kids. It was their bus, not ours, and they never let us forget it. And they didn't bother to speak to us.

"Kay's hands are red and chapped," Mary said. Only Mary could be so brave as to speak up like that. Elizabeth and my father barely spoke to one another. And when they did, it always went wrong.

Now, taking heart from Mary's bravery, Elizabeth came into the dining room.

"Daddy, everyone in our department at the arsenal is buying war bonds," she said.

"It isn't polite to interrupt, Elizabeth."

"Daddy, you know we never talk."

"If we don't, it's because you don't wish to, Elizabeth."

I saw tears in Elizabeth's eyes. But she kept on. "My supervisor called me in again yesterday and asked me why I wasn't having fifty cents a week taken out of my pay for war bonds. My supervisor said it was only patriotic."

"I can't afford patriotism," my father said.

"But, Daddy, Mary and I are the only ones not giving for war bonds. My supervisor thinks it's because I'm selfish."

"Let him think it, then." My father got up and went to the closet and took out his overcoat and fedora hat.

"*Her,* Daddy," Elizabeth said icily. "My supervisor is a woman."

My father waved his hand in disgust. "No wonder," he said. "Whenever women are in positions of authority they become troublemakers. I told you. I can't afford patriotism!" He yelled it.

"You can," I heard Elizabeth whisper as she went back into the kitchen. "Mary and

I turn in our whole paychecks every week."

If he heard her, my father ignored her. He turned to me instead. "If you can't ask for the mittens on the bus, you can go to school with chapped hands. It's March. Winter's almost over." And with that, he went out the door.

"What's all the noise? Can't a person sleep around here?" Amazing Grace came into the kitchen in her chenille bathrobe.

"Queenie's gone," Mary told her. "She ran off. Daddy's upset. But no reason for you to be upset, Mother. Here, sit down, we've got your breakfast all ready."

Amazing Grace took her place at the head of the table. Mary served her breakfast. Elizabeth stayed in the kitchen. She spoke to Amazing Grace even less than she spoke to my father.

"She never was any good," Amazing Grace said of Queenie. "It's best she's gone. She was sly and lazy. All coloreds are."

My face burned in shame. Not for what my stepmother said about Queenie, but because I didn't have the courage to defend her. Instead, I bent my head over my Wheatena, making myself invisible, as I always tried to do when Amazing Grace appeared.

I wanted to be like The Shadow on the radio. The Shadow could make himself invisible. "What evil lurks in the hearts of men?" the announcer always asked. "Only The Shadow knows."

Is it possible The Shadow is wrong? I asked myself. *I know that evil lurks in the hearts of women as well as men. Amazing Grace has evil in her heart. But The Shadow is one of my radio heroes. How can he be wrong?*

I brushed the thought aside. But I didn't defend Queenie. I just ate my cereal as quietly as I could. Because making myself invisible was becoming my best talent. All I had to do was sit very still and quiet and before I knew it, grown-ups forgot I even existed.

I watched Amazing Grace eat her eggs and bacon. The bacon smelled like all the things in the world I couldn't have. We weren't allowed bacon. Or chocolate Bosco to flavor our milk. Amazing Grace needed these things to make her strong for the baby. Even though she was plump and round already.

I was so skinny I could see my ribs through my skin, but nobody cared. Nazis were killing people in Europe. Why would anybody care about a little girl in New Jersey whose ribs showed and who had chapped hands?

My brothers came back downstairs, dressed for school, and took their places at the table.

"Martin, you're to go to the butcher shop after school," Amazing Grace said. "Kay, you're to go for eggs. To Mrs. Leudloff."

I stopped being invisible then and looked up. *Mrs. Leudloff?* We all stared at Amazing Grace. Even Elizabeth came in from the kitchen, though she didn't say anything.

"What's the matter?" Amazing Grace asked.

For once it wasn't Mary who spoke up. It was Martin. "Mrs. Leudloff is a German spy. She keeps a shortwave radio in her house."

Amazing Grace scowled. "Do you think that just because she's German, she's a spy?"

It was a trap. Amazing Grace often set traps for us. Her father was German, which made her half-German. Her mother was Austrian. Martin said Hitler was Austrian, too.

But Martin didn't flinch. "Everybody *knows* she has a shortwave radio. People have heard it."

"Who?" Amazing Grace demanded.

Martin played with his spoon in his cereal. "Mr. Schoenfeld, where we're supposed to go for eggs," he said.

"Mr. Schoenfeld is Jewish," Amazing Grace said. "So he hates all Germans. Mr. Schoenfeld is stupid. The reason Kay can't go there for eggs is because he got lime in his eye and is in the hospital. So today Kay goes to Mrs. Leudloff."

She had spoken. The matter was finished.

CHAPTER

3

Before they left the house, my sisters gave me advice about Mrs. Leudloff.

"Be polite," Mary said. "And don't tell her anything that goes on in this house. Don't dare mention that your sisters work in the arsenal!"

I promised I wouldn't. Mary had told me, on more than one occasion, that loose lips sink ships, that Nazis burn people in ovens, and that I am lucky to be a little girl living in America, rather than a little girl starving in Europe.

"Don't linger," was all Elizabeth said. Then she put her arm around me. And her arm around me was better than anything she could tell me.

On the long walk to get the school bus,

Martin had his own advice. "Going for eggs is better than going to the butcher shop. Sometimes I have to wait an hour in line. And all day, in school, I worry that I'll lose the coupons for meat. And sometimes I have to lug along that ball of fat to turn in. I hate it."

Turning in a ball of fat was part of the war effort. I don't know what they did with the fat. None of us did. We figured it was a military secret.

"Be careful of Rex, her Nazi dog," Tom said. "He'd just as soon bite your leg off as look at you. And listen for her short-wave radio. The FBI will want to know if you hear it."

I jingled the egg money that was wrapped in a handkerchief in my pocket. Usually I was nervous enough, carrying egg money around with me all day. Amazing Grace would kill me if I lost it. Now I had to worry about old German spy Mrs. Leudloff all day, too.

By the time I got on the bus my hands were freezing. But chapped hands could be hidden in my pockets, once I set my books and lunch box down. There was nowhere I could hide from the cold looks of the public-high-school girls.

I scrunched down into my seat. I knew I looked a sight in my blue serge uniform, my navy blue pea jacket, my cotton stockings held up with garters, and my clumsy brown laced-up oxford shoes.

The public-high-school girls wore neat pleated skirts, saddle shoes, and the whitest bobby socks. The white on their saddle shoes was buffed to a shine. The socks were rolled over twice. Under their coats they wore soft cashmere sweaters. Did one of them have my mittens? Why would they want them? They wore fashionable woolen or leather gloves.

I stared out the window. I hated traveling five miles on this bus every day to school. But my little country school had been closed down the Monday after the Japs bombed Pearl Harbor, a little over two years ago now. If I had no other reason to hate the Japs, that was enough.

I'd gone to school on Monday morning, the eighth of December, to find the doors locked. I'd stood crying in the schoolyard.

How could they close our school?

We had walked there every day, Martin, Tom, and I, past brooks and fields. It was not far from home.

I remember running around the school-yard that day looking for Martin. Mary and Elizabeth, of course, had been in high school. But Martin would know what was going on.

He did. "They're taking us away."

"Away? Where?" I asked. I knew a war had started. I knew the Japs had bombed Pearl Harbor the day before. I didn't even know where Pearl Harbor *was*. At first I thought it was on the river on the way to Waterville.

Is this what happens when a war starts? Immediately, they take the little kids away?

They loaded us onto yellow buses that day and took us on a two-mile ride to a strange school. Later on I found out they closed our school because it was across the street from the arsenal.

When we got to the new school, I knew there was a war on, all right. The kids there were lined up, waiting for us, in their schoolyard.

They all looked as mean as weasels. And they acted worse. They pushed, pinched, and shoved us, and said such terrible things that I began to wonder if the war hadn't really started a few miles away on the river.

Martin and Tom told my father, of course. And within weeks he took us out of that new school and put us in St. Bridget's.

I never did find out why those kids were so mean. I have discovered, since, that some people don't need a reason to be mean. That in itself is very scary.

"You'll have to wear a uniform now, Kay," my brothers told me when I started St. Bridget's.

I was glad for that. I pictured the uniform as being smart and sassy. I'd wear trousers with a stripe down the side. And a hat with a brim, like kids do in military school.

But my uniform is not smart and sassy. All it ended up being was dull and drab. A navy blue serge jumper and a white blouse. I hate it.

The kids in St. Bridget's are better, all except for the girls in the Golden Band. Whereas the kids in the last school were weasels, the girls in the Golden Band are only prigs.

I got through two years. I'm in fifth grade now. And Sister Brigitta runs the fifth grade like Hitler runs Germany.

In school Jennifer Bellows is my best friend.

At home there are no girls in the neighborhood to play with. I play with my brothers. I'm a fair hand at Cowboys and Indians. I can shoot marbles. I know to bump a player off the track and win an extra shot, and how to guard my puries in a marble game. And I'm right there helping Martin and Tom dam up the brook in summer.

At home I'd give my pea shooter for a girl best friend. So Jennifer is important to me.

We both have dark hair in a school that seems to be full of blond, blue-eyed girls who wear Mary Jane shoes and have lisps.

Jennifer is kind of a tomboy, too. We both wear brown oxfords, have older brothers, and bring lunch from home. All the other girls buy their lunches in the cafeteria, heaping plates of mashed potatoes with puddles of brown gravy, roast beef, and peas for ten cents a day. Chocolate milk is three cents.

My lunch is a peanut-butter sandwich in winter and tomatoes on soggy bread in spring and fall. To save money, the sandwich is wrapped in paper from Wonder bread.

I don't care that the other girls buy chocolate milk. Or that afterward they have money left to buy a Dixie cup. And they sit in front of me and lick ice cream off the photo of Judy Garland or Deanna Durbin inside the lid. But I'd give anything to have my sandwiches wrapped in real wax paper. Everybody stares at my Wonder-bread wrapping. And I feel poor.

Jennifer has sandwiches, too. Cream cheese. I think we became friends because neither of us is worthy enough to belong to the Golden Band.

They're the townie girls. They *walk* to school on tree-shaded streets. They live in identical two-story houses with wide porches. They listen to the same music, go to the same movies, and all wear their hair the same way: short and curled, with a little wave on top. They go to the same parties on weekends and wear Mary Janes.

My house is bigger than any of theirs, if you want to talk about houses. But that isn't the point. My house is five miles away, out in the country.

I don't belong. Neither does Jennifer, who also takes a bus to school, but from another direction.

To not-belong is bad. We're smart enough to know that.

But we're smarter not to try.

Jennifer's mother works as a nurse on the new-baby floor in the hospital. That's another fault. Nobody's mother works. Oh, I know lots of women work in war plants. Mary told me. But none of *these* girls' mothers work. So Jennifer has to peel potatoes and get the supper started when she goes home. My stepmother doesn't work, but I know about peeling potatoes. I guess Jennifer and I just found each other and clung to each other to stay alive.

As I stepped from the bus, I saw, right away, that there was a commotion in the schoolyard. Jennifer was surrounded by the Golden Band, and she was crying. I ran to her.

The Golden Band consisted of six girls: Cathy Doyle, Amy Crynan, Betsy Palmer, Eileen Keifer, Rosemary Winter, and Mary Ellen Bradley.

"What's wrong?" I asked.

"You mean you don't know, Kay?" Amy Crynan said it with contempt. As if I *should* know. They did. But everybody in the Golden Band always knew things I didn't know. Which was why I always felt so stupid around them.

Well, I was used to it. "No," I said.

"Her brother's ship was torpedoed by the Germans. He was lost at sea," Mary Ellen Bradley said.

Jennifer stood there and wailed louder and louder. Tears were streaming down her face. Deep sobs came up from her chest.

"Jen," I said. I tried to push my way through to her.

Her brother, Arthur, gone! I could not believe it.

"His ship was torpedoed by Hitler's Wolf Pack," Amy Crynan told everyone.

Here was something I knew. I knew about the Wolf Pack. They were Hitler's submarines. They called them U-boats. I'd seen them in movie newsreels that showed dead bodies floating in the ocean after one of our ships was torpedoed by them. Then, at the beach last summer, we'd seen tar and oil slicks on the sand from all the sunken ships.

"Jen!" I touched her.

But she didn't hear me. She was someplace else, in some terrible place where she was feeling a lot of pain. I could tell from the sound of her crying. It frightened me.

And then the Golden Band pushed me aside. They led Jennifer away. They walked with her into the school. Sister Mary Louise was ringing the cowbell that meant classes were starting.

They would announce over the loud-speaker that Jennifer Bellows's brother had been lost in the war. And we'd pray for him.

I stood alone in the cold schoolyard, wondering whose loose lips had sunk the ship Jennifer's brother had been on. And how I was going to survive in school without Jennifer for a friend.

Because I knew she was gone from me. Before this day the girls in the Golden Band would never have bothered with her. She wasn't a townie. She ate cream-cheese sandwiches, she wore brown oxfords, her mother worked.

But today she had something nobody else had. A brother killed in the war.

The nuns would coddle and pet her. She'd be the center of attention in school. She was important now. And worthy, finally, of the Golden Band.

She was as gone from me as Queenie was. I'd lost another friend.

Who will I have now? I asked myself. *Lucy Spinella?* She's Spanish and dark-skinned and poor. She stays to herself. The girls laugh at her. Once one of them touched her kerchief by mistake and ran, screaming, to wash her hands.

Paula Karchup? She's even worse off. She doesn't even *have* lunch. She sits at the far end of the cafeteria with her hands folded in front of her, saying, "I'm not hungry." Every day she says that. Nobody bothers to ask why she doesn't have lunch or why she isn't hungry.

I have nobody now, I thought. I'll walk alone, like it says in that song my sister Mary sings. Or like Bulldog Drummond, the detective who comes on the radio Tuesday evenings, I'll make lonely footsteps in the night, coming out of the fog. Then what will I do?

I don't know, I decided. I'm not allowed to stay up to hear the whole show. So I don't know what happens to Bulldog Drummond when he walks alone in the fog. I'll just have to make up the rest as I go along.

Oh, Queenie, how will I keep smiling through?

CHAPTER

4

I couldn't get Jennifer out of my mind all day.

Sister Brigitta smacked me on the hand with the ruler four times because I couldn't remember how much nine times three was. She stood over me with that ruler while I recited the times tables. I was so scared that my mind went blank after nine times two. Then I started to cry, and she hit my hands and made me sit in the corner with a dunce cap on.

Jennifer wasn't in class. Where was she? She finally arrived in time for the afternoon classes. Cathy Doyle whispered that she'd been in the nurse's office.

Before we started, Sister Brigitta asked Jennifer who she wanted to go to the office with her, to lead the prayer for her brother over the loudspeaker.

I was back in my seat by then. It was such an honor to go to the office and lead the prayers! I'd never been picked. I never thought I could do it if Sister sent me. But I'd do it for Jennifer. But Jennifer looked right past me.

"Amy Crynan," Jennifer said.

My heart sank.

Amy was the leader of the Golden Band. Her hair was blond and she was perfect in every way. I always felt like an insect next to Amy.

I wanted to die. It hurt worse than Sister Brigitta's ruler as I watched Jennifer and Amy walk out of the class, hand in hand.

"Boys and girls." Sister Mary Louise's voice was soft and serious over the loudspeaker. "Amy Crynan will now lead the grammar school in prayer for Arthur Bellows, whose ship was torpedoed by the Germans and whose soul is now with God. As you know, his sister, Jennifer, is in Sister Brigitta's fifth grade."

His soul with God. It gave me the shivers. But it must be true. And Arthur Bellows must have some influence with God, too, I decided. Because Amy never got to say those prayers.

Just then we heard the sirens for an air-raid drill. For the *whole* school, not just the grammar. St. Bridget's Junior High and High School were scattered through our building and the building next door.

Immediately we dived under the desks, while the sirens kept on and on. We had to cross our legs and put our hands together over our heads and keep very quiet and still.

The sirens made a lonely, frightening sound. I looked across the aisle at Jennifer's empty desk. *Your brother is punishing you, Jen,* I thought, *because you didn't pick me to lead the prayers. And he's with God. So you better watch out.*

The minute I opened the gate at Mrs. Leudloff's house her German shepherd went crazy. He snarled and barked and his fangs dripped, just like some creature on the scariest radio program we listened to, *Inner Sanctum Mysteries.*

Mrs. Leudloff kept him in a fenced-in place in the middle of the yard. Which meant I had to get by him in order to get to another gate, where I would have to ring a small bell to tell her I wanted eggs.

I'd seen Nazi dogs in newsreels at the movies. And Rex acted as fierce as any of them. I kept as far from him as I could as I raced to the second gate. Then I rang the bell.

The back door of the neat white clapboard house opened and Mrs. Leudloff came out. She had light brown, fluffy, short hair and a belted jacket, and she wore gray slacks. There was a bounce in her step and she was very slim and cheerful.

"Yes?" she asked.

"I need some eggs, Mrs. Leudloff."

"Come, come. Glad to see you."

She couldn't fool me with that nice smile. Or pull the wool over my eyes with her stylish hair or slim waist. *I don't trust happy and cheerful anyway,* I thought. *Life is serious and hard.* In school, when the nuns want to be nice, they read to us about the Christians who got eaten by the lions in Rome.

As for my egg buying, I was used to Mrs. Schoenfeld, short and dumpy. Her house was cavernous and messy and dark. She was Jewish. She sang opera while she boxed the eggs for me. Everybody in operas either dies in the end or gets stabbed. My sister Mary says Mrs. Schoenfeld knows about sorrow, being Jewish. And that she has culture.

"One dozen?" Mrs. Leudloff asked.

"Yes, please."

She began to fill an egg carton. "How are your parents?"

"Fine, thank you."

"And school? Do you study hard?"

"Yes."

"Good. The new baby comes soon?"

"In late spring, I think." Oh, I knew Mary warned me not to tell her anything that goes on in our house. But what could I do? This lady was so cheerful.

"You want a brother or a sister?"

What I wanted had nothing to do with anything. I wanted bacon for breakfast, chocolate syrup in my milk, Mary Janes. I wanted Queenie back and Jennifer for a friend again. I would get none of these things, so what was the sense in wanting?

Besides, at home we never spoke of the baby, except for how we must take care of Amazing Grace. Its coming was a private matter. But Mrs. Leudloff was waiting for my answer.

"I'd like a little sister," I said.

She smiled. "Of course you would. I hear Queenie left."

"You know Queenie?"

"She came here for eggs once or twice. We became friends. I didn't think she'd stay at your house very long."

"My father is going to get someone else."

Her light blue eyes looked into mine. "Not Tony and Marie."

"Why?"

"They worked here once. I had to let them go. Now all I have is Mr. Jesco. But he's a good worker." She shook her head. "I don't usually say things against people. We must all learn to be kind to each other these days. Just tell your father, if he hires them, not to leave his children unsupervised."

I took the eggs and handed her the money.

"My, look at those chapped hands. Where are your mittens?"

"I lost them."

"Wait. I have an old pair around."

"No, ma'am, I couldn't."

"You wait!" She said it sternly.

I stood there in the cold yard. Rex was sitting in his fenced-in place, growling at me. I wanted to go. It was cold. I had another mile to walk yet. And I wanted to get home to listen to our radio programs. But Mrs. Leudloff had said to wait, and I was taught to obey.

The back door slammed again, and she came bouncing out. "Here." She thrust a pair of blue mittens at me.

I looked at them in the same way I'd looked at the bacon at breakfast. "I couldn't take them," I said.

"Why? Nobody's using them."

I was confused. *Why is she being so nice?* I wondered. *She isn't supposed to be nice. She's German, isn't she?* I shook my head. "They wouldn't like it at home."

"So? Do you have to tell them?"

Not tell them? It was unthinkable. I didn't even know how to consider such a thing. "Thank you just the same," I said.

She put the mittens in her coat pocket. "Then have some candy." From her other pocket she took some wrapped taffy and hard candy. "Go ahead. All my customers get candy."

I accepted some, thanked her, and crept past Rex, who once again started to lunge at the white picket-fence enclosure.

"Don't be afraid, he wouldn't hurt you," she said.

I was not afraid. I was terrified. Somehow

I got out the front gate and onto the road. She waved. I started to walk down the hill.

The candy was delicious. I felt so guilty eating it. I seldom got candy. But this I could keep from them at home. Because it would be gone before I got there. And I deserved something for putting up with Rex, didn't I?

I turned once, to look up at the house. I'd forgotten to listen for the shortwave radio!

"Maybe you'll take the mittens next time," she called out.

There would be no next time, candy or no candy, I told myself. Mrs. Schoenfeld couldn't stay away from the egg farm more than one day, even if her husband had hurt his eye. Only Mrs. Leudloff didn't know that.

CHAPTER

5

Hop Harrigan was just asking, on the radio, for clearance to land, when I came in the door.

His voice was·calling the central tower on his plane's radio. The Ace of the Airwaves was starting another adventure. He and his pal, Tank Tinker, were always on dangerous missions behind enemy lines.

It's my job to make tea for Grace, my brothers, and myself when I get home from school. I hurried to the kitchen.

That's one good thing about Amazing Grace; she loves her afternoon tea. It's because she's English. At least that's what she tells us. Since her father is German and her mother Austrian, I don't know how she got to be English. But with the war, you never know.

People change with the war. Look at Kato, Britt Reid's houseboy on *The Green Hornet.* He was Japanese before the war. Now he's Filipino.

Amazing Grace was sitting in the dining room at her Singer sewing machine, putting the finishing touches on the jumper she was making for me. Martin and Tom were on the floor in front of the radio.

Amazing Grace had the water boiling and the toast in the toaster. I got out the butter and jam, put it all on a tray, managed to pour the water in the pot without burning my hands, and carried the tray to the dining-room table.

Amazing Grace watched as I set the tray down. She'd be on me in a minute if I spilled anything, slapping with her sharp hand. I was used to it. She was a stepmother, and stepmothers did that sort of thing. I was luckier than Snow White, after all. Her step-mother had ordered the huntsman to cut out her heart.

"Did you get the eggs?"

"Yes. I put them in the ice box."

"Well, Mr. Schoenfeld came home from the hospital this afternoon. He may be blind in one eye."

I didn't know what to say to that. She

acted as if it was my fault. So I said nothing.

"So your father will want you to buy eggs from him. He'll need our business. Now have your tea, then go and change. I want you to peel potatoes for supper. I can't do everything around here, and your sisters don't get home until late."

I took my tea, toast, and jam and sat under the dining-room table. The lace cloth came halfway down, and I felt in a world of my own. The boys had grabbed their tea and toast and were glued to the radio.

Hop Harrigan was fighting madmen again. The world was full of madmen. They frothed at the mouth, they laughed like hyenas, and they plotted to take over the planet.

After Hop Harrigan came *Captain Midnight,* then *The Lone Ranger,* then *Jack Armstrong, the All American Boy.* There were plenty of madmen for all of them to handle.

That afternoon, however, my mind wasn't on Hop's problems but on my own. And by the time Glenn Riggs, the announcer, was reminding us at the end of the program to save and turn in waste fats and bring paper, tin, and rubber to the salvage depots, and how badly the Red Cross needed blood, I'd made up my mind.

I wouldn't tell anyone how Mrs. Leudloff

had given me candy. What I'd had that afternoon was an adventure.

Everybody was having adventures these days, from Captain Midnight to The Shadow. And one thing I'd noticed about them all: They had secrets. Things they didn't tell anybody.

Captain Midnight's job in the war was so important that not even his superiors knew his identity. The Shadow had a hypnotic power to cloud men's minds. He'd learned it in the Orient.

I have a right to an adventure, I told myself. *And a secret.* Being a Catholic, I had to tell everything to the priest once a month, in confession. Secrets were forbidden to me.

But I hadn't stolen the candy, so I didn't do anything wrong. I had a real secret. For the first time in my life.

And Mrs. Leudloff had given it to me. The feeling was delicious. Almost as good as the candy.

Tony and Marie came to our back door that night just as Henry Aldrich's mother, on the radio, was calling him to come home. My sisters were listening in the dining room as they set their hair at the table.

One of Amazing Grace's rules was that
none of us were allowed to stay in our bed-
rooms for anything but dressing and sleeping. "Anything else you can do right down
here," she'd told Elizabeth and Mary. "I'm
not going to have any girlish daydreaming
in my house. It only leads to trouble."

We were allowed no privacy to think or
read alone, any of us. Reading was a waste
of time, Amazing Grace said. Idle hands
were the devil's workshop.

So there were my sisters, with towels
around their shoulders, setting their hair at
the dining-room table, when Tony and Marie came into the kitchen to speak to my
father.

Tom and Martin and I were on the stairs
in the center hall, half listening to Henry Aldrich and half listening to the conversation
in the kitchen.

"No drinking, Tony," I heard my father
say. "I won't have drinking if you come work
for me."

"I don't drink no more, mister," Tony
said.

I could see him standing there with his
hat in his hand, just like he'd done last
Christmas Eve when he'd come to my father

and said, "Mister, I need to borrow some money. I have to buy my kids some presents."

"If you'd stop drinking . . . ," my father had told him that day. Then he'd given Tony a lecture about drinking. I remember thinking that if Tony was my father I wouldn't want any presents if he had to listen to a lecture to get money to buy them.

"He needs money," Martin whispered to me. "I heard he was fired at the diner."

Tony washed dishes at the diner up on Route 6. He was very ragged. His eyes were red, and he wasn't shaved.

"Gosh all hemlock," I said.

"Will you stop talking like Betty on *Jack Armstrong?*" Tom complained.

Betty was the only girl in the cast of the show. I liked her because, like me, she was always waiting in agony for some important outcome.

"I'm afraid of Tony," I whispered to Tom. "He looks like an enemy of the free world. Are they going to live here?"

"Nah," Martin said. "They only live across the highway. They'll come every day."

Marie wore high-laced boots and layers of clothing. She didn't look as if she could tap dance.

"Kay, go get your teddy bear," Martin said.

"Not now, Martin."

"Go get him. I need a smoke."

Ope, my teddy bear, had a mouth that opened. Martin borrowed cigarettes from Amazing Grace and told her he put them in Ope's mouth to pretend the bear was smoking. Amazing Grace was awful stupid sometimes. She believed him.

Though Martin was only fourteen, he'd been smoking for two years already. He said that everybody who was grown up and important smoked. On *Your Hit Parade*, they told us how many cartons of cigarettes were sent to wounded soldiers in hospitals overseas. And how the new Lucky Strike package would only be red and white now, because the green from the package had gone to war.

"Some night you're going to burn the house down," I told Martin. But I started upstairs to get Ope.

Later that night I lay in bed in my little room, staring at the ceiling and listening to the grown-up talk from below. Soon the conversation died down and I heard my father banking the fire in the kitchen stove and locking the doors.

"Go to sleep, girls," my father told my

sisters as he and Amazing Grace were coming up the stairs.

"After *Inner Sanctum*," Mary said.

And then I heard the squeaking door of *Inner Sanctum* and the announcer inviting my sisters through the squeaking door. Then he said something about werewolves and laughed crazily.

I wasn't afraid of werewolves, even though it was dark in my room. How could I be afraid of something they made up for radio programs when the world was full of madmen killing people? But I missed Ope, who was with Martin now. I missed Queenie, and I felt sad. The world was a sad place.

If it wasn't, I would have been allowed to take those mittens from Mrs. Leudloff so my hands wouldn't freeze. I would *have* new mittens, even though I'd lost my others.

I hugged Mary Frances, my rubber baby doll. Mary had told me that my mother had held me only once before she'd died. "She had a long name picked out for you," Mary said. "But she said you were so little, she had to name you Kay."

Kay, not even Katherine. And Kay, not even with an E on the end.

"What was the name she had picked out?" I asked Mary.

But she said she didn't know. So it could be anything. It could be Victoria. Or Eugenia. Or Constance. Lovely names. *I would make a wonderful Constance,* I thought.

When I was seven I decided the name would have been Mary Frances. Two names, both strong and true. The girls in the Golden Band would respect me if my name were Mary Frances, I was sure of it. That was Francie's real name in *A Tree Grows in Brooklyn,* wasn't it?

So that was the name I'd given to my rubber baby doll. I fell asleep holding her tight.

I didn't have to peel potatoes when I got home from school anymore, now that Marie was in the kitchen. For the next few days I was freed from that task. In our house, for a short time, there was order, with Marie in the kitchen and Tony in the yard.

But only for a very short time.

On Saturday, Mary took me into town for shoes. All the way in on the number 4 bus, Mary read. She was always reading, though Amazing Grace didn't like it.

"What are you reading?" I asked. I don't like sitting on the bus with somebody and having that somebody not talk to me. I do that all week with the public-high-school girls.

"*Great Expectations*," she said. "It's by Charles Dickens."

"What's it about?"

"A little boy who gets treated very mean by an old lady."

"Why do you have to read that? We know all about being treated mean in our house."

Mary made her lips tight. "Don't talk bad about our family," she said.

"Well, there isn't anything good to say, is there?"

"Then don't say anything at all."

I kept quiet all the rest of the bus ride into town. Sometimes I just don't understand Mary. Amazing Grace is almost as bad to her as she is to the rest of us. But Mary won't complain. She won't talk against Amazing Grace, either. She pretends we're a happy family. Because that's the way she wants us to be. Pretending doesn't make it so. And I wonder if Mary knows that.

She fawns over Amazing Grace, too. Not that it gets her much more than the rest of us get. Mary isn't allowed to have bacon or chocolate syrup, either. But Amazing Grace is a little nicer to her than she is to the rest of us.

Well, I don't care. I'm like Elizabeth. I won't fawn over anybody to get treated a little nicer. I'd rather be treated mean and say what I feel.

I got my Mary Janes that Saturday in town. Mary took me right into Carver's Department Store, where they have sparkling things behind glass counters. And salesladies in fluffy blouses. We walked through to the shoe department and right there, where I knew that Cathy Doyle and Amy Crynan got their Mary Janes, I got mine.

For once I didn't get Buster Brown oxfords. I couldn't believe it! The Mary Janes were so shiny, I could see my face in them. And when I walked across the carpet so the salesman could see how they fit, I felt as if I could tap-dance right there. I was so happy, I felt tears in my eyes. And I forgave Mary for fawning over Amazing Grace. Because if anybody could convince Amazing Grace that I should have these shoes, it was Mary. Nobody else.

Afterward, clutching the shoe box close, I

followed Mary while we shopped. We had some things to get for Amazing Grace. Then Mary took me to Hooper's Drugstore for an ice cream soda.

The sun shone warm that late March afternoon. The world seemed a bright bubble as I sat in a leather booth, looking out the clear glass window of Hooper's, and sipped my soda.

People were shopping for Easter, which was two weeks away. I would have Mary Janes for Easter! *Oh, Queenie,* I thought, *you were wrong! I can have Mary Janes! And I will be a tap dancer!*

I didn't even mind that Mary didn't talk to me much but kept right on reading Charles Dickens while she sipped her coffee across the table from me. I was as close to being happy as I ever remember being in my life.

It didn't last.

I should have known it wouldn't last. The sky clouded over on the walk home from the bus stop. And when we got into the house, Amazing Grace and my father were just returning home from the market with the week's groceries.

Nothing put them both in a bad mood

more than shopping for groceries. Gloom descended over everything.

"Such money spent!" Amazing Grace was complaining. "And you children don't appreciate the fact that your father buys all this food for you. Did Elizabeth clean out the refrigerator?"

But Elizabeth was not to be found.

"Everything is so expensive! And we can't even get decent vegetables! I'm exhausted! Where's Marie?"

"She has the afternoon off," Martin said.

"Already?" Amazing Grace glared at me. "That lazy thing, taking a day off already. Nobody wants to work anymore."

I felt guilty. Surely, somehow it was all my fault—the high prices, the lack of vegetables, the unclean refrigerator, and the fact that nobody wanted to work anymore.

"Help your mother," my father scolded. Then he left the room, went across the hall into his library, and closed the door.

We all jumped into action. Martin ran for the rest of the grocery bags. Mary put on the kettle for tea. I started to put some boxes of dry food away, and Tom took the milk pail and went out to milk the cow.

"What's in the package?" Amazing Grace said, eyeing my shoe box on the chair.

"Kay's new shoes," Mary said.

"Well, I hope they fit right. They have to last. Let me see them."

From the stove, Mary half turned to look at me. "Open the box," she said. But her voice was dead when she said it, and my heart sank.

I'd thought Mary would make everything all right with the shoes. She could always get around Amazing Grace. Why was her voice so dead? She wouldn't let me down, would she? Not Mary! She could always work some kind of magic with our stepmother.

Amazing Grace untied the string and took off the lid. Then she gasped. "Mary Janes! Why Mary Janes?"

Mary was getting the tea out of the pantry. "Easter is coming. She's a little girl."

Amazing Grace scowled. Her mouth dropped at the corners. Her eyes went narrow. "You begged Mary for these, didn't you?" she said to me.

I didn't answer.

She grabbed me by the arms then and shook me. "I'll give you Mary Janes," she said angrily. "Your father works so hard. I

give up so much. And you think you're going to wear Mary Janes?"

But I couldn't answer, she was shaking me
so hard.

"Who do you think you *are* that you
should wear Mary Janes?" She growled it at
me. Like Rex the dog.

"Mother, don't!" Mary cried. "It was my
fault, not hers."

"Go clean out the refrigerator!" she ordered.

Mary did so.

"Who?" Amazing Grace screamed it.

"Nobody." I got the word out finally. "I'm
nobody."

Satisfied, she released me and slammed
the cover down on the box. "Mary, you're to
take these shoes back. Next Saturday. And
get brown oxfords. Do you hear?"

"Yes, Mother," Mary said meekly.

"Go set the table for supper!" Amazing
Grace shoved me.

I went, sobbing. How could the beautiful
bubble that had been my afternoon have
broken so? Worse yet, how could I have
been deceived by it, and think it wouldn't?

CHAPTER
6

Things started to go real wrong from that Saturday on. And I guess Queenie was right. I never should have gotten those Mary Janes. Bad things would happen if I did.

First, Tony turned up missing. There was no real connection between him and my shoes, but the way I was thinking, I figured there must be.

It happened Monday after school. Amazing Grace was napping; Marie was in the kitchen preparing supper. I went into the dining room to join my brothers at the radio.

"Where's Martin?" I asked Tom.

"Collecting scrap for the scrap drive."

"Why aren't you helping?"

"I've got to milk the cow as soon as our programs are over."

"I thought that's Tony's job now."

"He's hiding."

"Why?"

"He chased me around the barn with a knife this morning."

I just stared at my brother. Sometimes he made things up, like I did. Listening to our radio programs all the time, it wasn't hard to make things up. "You're lying," I said.

"I'm not. He's hiding because if Daddy finds out, he'll lose his job."

"Why did he chase you?"

"He was starting to milk Daisy. I went out to see if everything was okay. It wasn't. He was hitting her in the face because she wouldn't stand still for him. I told him to stop."

"Poor Daisy! What did you do?"

"I yelled at him and made him stop. Then I ran. He chased me with the knife and warned me not to tell Dad."

"Are you going to tell?"

"I don't know," he said. "I don't like the way he treats Daisy, but I'm sick and tired of having to get up so early to milk her all the time. If he stays, I don't have to."

I sat under the table thinking. *Gosh all hemlock.* Mrs. Leudloff said my father

shouldn't leave us unsupervised around
Tony and Marie. She'd *known* something!
How? Was it because she had a shortwave
radio?

Would Tom tell my father about Tony? I
knew he had to get up awfully early to milk
Daisy. But it wasn't right she should be hit
like that. She was a good cow.

Then it came to me that Tom could have
been killed, if Tony had caught up with him
with that knife.

*Tony was a dangerous person to have
around.* Madmen were not only the Japanese
and the Germans, but sometimes right here
in the middle of us all. Sometimes they were
Americans!

What would Tom do?

I didn't hear half of *Hop Harrigan,* for wor-
rying about that. Finally I set my cup down
on the floor, curled up on the rug, and went
to sleep under the table.

Tonto's voice woke me. "Me, Kemo Sabe,"
he was saying to the Lone Ranger.

Then came the Lone Ranger's voice, deep,
calming. "You've been a faithful friend to me,
Tonto."

The Lone Ranger is tough and hard, with
an iron will and an unswerving sense of justice. What would *he* do about Tony?

Well, I knew that. He'd bring justice to Tony all by himself. Everything would be all right when he got finished.

"Me and Martin sent Wheaties box tops and a dime each for pedometers from the *Jack Armstrong* show," Tom told me.

"Where did you get a dime each?"

"From our allowances."

The boys got fifteen cents each, every week, for an allowance. I wasn't old enough yet.

"What are the pedometers for?"

"They can plot the location of hidden caches of rifles. Or keep you safe when you're trekking through Africa. They're magic."

"I want a luminous bracelet, like Betty wears."

"One of us will let you borrow our pedometer. Do you know that you have to say the Pledge of Allegiance at the Farmers Co-operative meeting tonight?"

"Who said so?"

"Amazing Grace. And you've got to wear the new jumper she made you."

Amazing Grace couldn't sew to save her soul, as Queenie had once said. Nothing she made turned out right. She either put ruffles on everything or made me look like a nun.

The last dress she'd made me was navy blue taffeta with a high neck and long sleeves. It made me look as if I was going to a funeral.

The new jumper was bright yellow flannel with ruffles on the shoulders. It was trimmed with blue rickrack. It was overdone and ridiculous. She'd patterned it after something Judy Garland had worn in a movie.

"I can't get up there in that jumper. I'd rather wear my school uniform," I said.

"You have to, or she'll be hurt," Tom said.

"I'll look silly. Everybody will laugh at me."

"I'll cloud their minds, like The Shadow does. So they won't see the jumper."

I laughed. "You can't do that."

"Yes, I can." He stood up and put on his jacket. "I clouded Tony's mind. How else do you think I got away from him?"

I wondered if I should worry about Tom. He was getting almost as bad as I was over our radio programs. Boys weren't supposed to be that way. Sister Brigitta said that people who wanted to be like movie or radio stars were confused about life.

I didn't have to think much to know why we were confused. It was because we'd lost our mother. But not only that, we were never allowed to speak of her. It made Amazing Grace crazy if anyone so much as mentioned her name. There were no pictures of her around anywhere.

"Are you going to tell Dad about Tony?" I asked Tom as he got ready to leave.

He zipped up his jacket. "Yeah."

"Why? Then he'll fire Tony. And you'll have to get up early and milk the cow again."

He grinned. "Yeah, I know. But at least I know Daisy won't be hit in the face by Tony anymore. I have to think of that, too."

I decided that I didn't have to worry about Tom. He wasn't confused. I didn't know if he could cloud people's minds tonight so they wouldn't see my awful jumper. But his own mind wasn't clouded, I knew that much, for sure.

CHAPTER

7

Even though he went to New York every day to work in an insurance company as an executive, my father considered himself a farmer.

Our big, rambling, thirteen-room house sat on five acres. About a quarter of an acre was a vegetable garden every summer. Everybody had vegetable gardens, on account of the war. They called them victory gardens. But my father didn't have his garden for victory. He had it and our farm so that he could go to regular meetings at the local Farmers Cooperative, where he could talk about things like crop rotation and how to get rid of potato bugs and the right way to keep chickens.

I liked going to these meetings because

they had soda and cupcakes for the kids. I didn't like wearing that yellow flannel jumper, though. Everyone stared at me in it. Most of the schoolgirls had plaid skirts, white blouses, and Mary Janes.

"And now," said Mr. Murphy, the president of the cooperative, as he quieted the people in the hall, "Kay Hennings will say the Pledge of Allegiance."

My knees shook as I walked up to the stage. *I hope you can cloud their minds, Tom,* I thought. Then, just as I got to the stairs, there was a commotion to one side of the hall.

Two men were arguing. "Don't you ever say a thing like that in my presence again!" said a tall man with glasses.

"I only said the war has made my egg business better," said a short one with bald hair and a patch over one eye.

Up on the stage I could see over everyone's head. And I gasped at what I saw.

Mr. Vineland was coming near to blows with Mr. Schoenfeld, who wore a patch over his eye.

"My son is serving on an aircraft carrier!" Mr. Vineland was shouting. His fists were clenched. Two other men had to hold him back. "And my daughter Beverly's fiancée is a paratrooper. I don't want to hear what money you're making on the war!"

"Gentlemen, gentlemen!" Mr. Murphy walked over to them. "Let us remember that we must pull together, here on the home front."

"Daddy, Daddy." Beverly Vineland ran up to her father. "Come on, Daddy, don't." She was crying.

Mr. Schoenfeld looked pale. "I just lost my eye in the war effort."

"You lost your eye because you're stupid," Mr. Vineland told him. "Because you don't know how to work with lime."

Mr. Schoenfeld was shaking. "Before the war," he told Mr. Murphy and the others, "his son didn't have a job. Now he has a chance to travel and is learning to be a radio operator."

"I'd rather have my son home!" Mr. Vineland shouted. "What do you know? You have two daughters!"

"Get my coat, Leonora," Mr. Schoenfeld said. "We don't need to stay and be insulted."

His wife got both their coats. Beverly and Mrs. Vineland sat down with Mr. Vineland.

Mr. Murphy was running after Mr. Schoenfeld, begging him to stay. But they left.

A murmuring went through the crowd.

"Kay, say the Pledge of Allegiance," Mr. Murphy directed, striding back to the stage.

I said it, but nobody was paying me much mind. Oh, they stood with their hands over their hearts. But they were not looking at me or my ridiculous yellow jumper. It was the furthest thing from their minds. I don't even think they heard my voice at all.

Grateful, I walked off the stage and back into the audience.

The crowd sat down, and the murmuring began again. All night they talked about the argument between two good Farmers Cooperative members.

They talked about it at tables where sample cakes, made with little or no sugar, were set out. They talked about it as local high school students recited how they were learning Junior Red Cross first aid or going into the Junior Air Reserve.

They talked about it when Mrs. Burton got up and told the women to be extra brave and proud and to have faith, even as they did away with the fripperies in their lives.

"Ladies," she finished, "plan your meals

carefully. Don't forget, darling dresses can be made out of feed bags. Keep your courage high and your lipstick handy."

Everyone gave her a round of applause. Then they went back to talking about the fight.

Was Mr. Vineland right in saying that making money on the war was wrong? Or was Mr. Schoenfeld right? He had stepped up his egg production to keep up with the war need.

The Lone Ranger would know, with his unswerving sense of justice; I was sure of it. But the Lone Ranger wasn't here. Only our plain, ordinary neighbors and my family were here.

As we put our coats on, Beverly Vineland came up to us. "Please don't think harshly of my father, Mr. Hennings. He worries so about Harry. And my Al."

"Does it matter what I think, Beverly?"

"Yes. Everybody in the neighborhood looks up to you. You've got the biggest house and the best job. You go into New York every day. You know what's going on. We're sure you have some answers."

She was looking at him as if he were the Lone Ranger. *He doesn't have any answers,* I wanted to yell at her. *You should see how con-fused things are in our house!*

Still, my father got all puffed up and im-portant looking when she said that. Eliza-beth would say it was his executive look. "Well, I'll tell you one thing that's going on, Beverly. Every day in Penn Station I see young boys going off to war. I see them say-ing good-bye to their families. It's awful," my father said, "just awful. And you're a good girl to stick up for your father. From now on we buy our eggs from Mrs. Leudloff."

She got tears in her eyes. "Thank you, Mr. Hennings. You've always been a good neighbor."

"What do you hear from Al?" my father asked.

"He's well, and they're shipping him to a different place. But he doesn't know where. And did I tell you, Mrs. Hennings?" She looked at Amazing Grace. "When he comes home, he's bringing his parachute. I'm going to have my wedding gown made out of it."

"That's nice." Amazing Grace sniffed. "Did you see the jumper I made Kay?"

"Yes," Beverly said weakly.

"Nobody even noticed it." Grace's nose was out of joint.

"Well, golly gee willikers," Beverly said, "everybody's making their own clothes these days. Tell Mary I've got some new Glenn Miller records. And I'm on day shifts next week. So we can listen to them, evenings." She worked for the telephone company.

"I'm going to make Kay a dress out of feed-bag material. She'll be wearing it to the next meeting," Amazing Grace told her.

My heart fell inside me. The bags our cow feed came in were a kind of strong muslin, printed with flowers. *Now I have to have a feed-bag dress?*

I knew why. Amazing Grace couldn't stand to be bested by anybody. If Beverly could make her wedding gown out of her boyfriend's silk parachute, Amazing Grace would make me a feed-bag dress. Well, I wouldn't wear it. Everybody *knows* feed-bag material when they see it. It means you're poor and can't afford to buy fabric, I don't care what they say about being patriotic.

I knew my father wasn't poor. Stingy, yes, but not poor.

In the worn backseat of our '38 Oldsmobile, Martin nudged me. "You've got to go back to the old Nazi spy now for eggs. Just because Mr. Schoenfeld bragged how much money he's making on the war."

"I heard it," I said.

"I told you I'd cloud their minds when you got up to say the Pledge of Allegiance, didn't I?" Tom whispered.

"You're right, Tom." I answered. "You did real good. They hardly even looked at me."

CHAPTER
8

All that spring I went to Mrs. Leudloff for eggs. It had nothing to do with Mrs. Leudloff herself. I was sent because Mr. Schoenfeld and Mr. Vineland had had a fight. Mary said it was because our father had to show his support for Mr. Vineland, whose son was fighting the war.

I thought it strange that we should support the war effort by buying eggs from a German lady instead of a Jewish man. But that year everything seemed strange. And kept right on getting stranger.

The morning after the Farmers Cooperative meeting, Tony still couldn't be found. Neither could my jar of sugar.

Because there was such a shortage of sugar, in our house we each had our own jar with our name on it. Every month the jar was filled up. It wasn't a big jar, either. So if you used too much on your cereal, you went without until the next month's supply came through.

All the jars were kept in the kitchen pantry.

My jar was missing. Along with Tony, who hadn't showed up for chores since he chased Tom with the knife.

That did it for my father. That plus the fact that Marie had broken a pink glass dish in the china closet the night before. Nobody ever said so, but I think those dishes belonged to my own mother. Amazing Grace doesn't like them. She never uses them. And once she and my father had a fight about keeping them there in the china closet. She wanted them out. He said they stayed. And they did.

That morning my father told Marie that she and Tony would have to leave.

"Wherever we go it is always the same," she said. "My man gets into trouble."

I felt sorry for Marie. But I just sat there at the table, staring at my Wheatena and wondering how I would eat it without my sugar. Wheatena was good for you; it was hard to take without sugar.

"Maybe your brothers and sisters will help

out until we get next month's supply," my father said as he went into the hall to get his coat and hat.

They did. They each gave me two precious spoonfuls. They filled half my new little jar.

Amazing Grace didn't offer any of hers.

When my father came back into the kitchen with his fedora hat and coat on, he looked pleased. But he didn't stay that way long. He never did. Soon enough, he looked serious.

"I have an announcement," he said.

We all got quiet.

"Your mother needs help with the house. And no one seems to be working out. So we're going to have Nana and Grandpa come until the baby arrives. And for a while after."

Everybody started talking at once then. Elizabeth said Nana was too old. Mary said, "Now Kay will have to move into our room." She didn't seem pleased about it.

Martin said Grandpa would teach him to play poker. Tom said, "Well, I guess I'll have to keep milking Daisy. Grandpa won't do that."

My father looked like the Germans were in our apple orchard. He couldn't wait to catch the 7:35 and be out of there.

I ran into the little back hallway as he left. "Daddy."

He turned. "I'm late now. What is it?"

"Do I have to wear a dress made of feed bags?"

"If your mother makes it, you'll wear it, Kay. She's doing her best. We all are." And he went out the door.

Nana and Grandpa are Amazing Grace's parents. They live in a little rowhouse in Brooklyn. It has a sunporch where a bird in a standing cage lives, a parlor with a piano, a small dining room and kitchen, and an even smaller backyard.

To get there, we have to take the train to New York first, then the subway that goes miles underground. The cars shake and screech and bang. The lights go off and on. Then suddenly we come out into the bright sunlight of Brooklyn, where we have to take a bus, then walk about four blocks.

I like going there. Brooklyn has neat little houses. Nana sends us out to the corner deli for cold cuts for lunch and makes pot roast for supper. We can make faces at the kids next door and they can make faces at us.

Of course, we don't dream of playing

together. Grown-ups think kids just play when they don't even know each other. But they don't. There are certain rules that apply before you can play together, certain things you have to do. One of those things is making faces. We kids all know that. And if grown-ups don't, well, that's their problem. We don't have to tell them everything, do we?

"Well, John," Nana always says at supper, halfway between the pot roast and dessert, "and how is business?"

You can count on her saying it. And when she does, I know dessert is coming soon.

If we go on Saturday, my father always takes Mary, Elizabeth, Tom, and Martin to Coney Island while Amazing Grace visits with her mother. I cry because I want to go to Coney Island, too. But my father says I'm too little.

These times, Nana takes me on her lap and tells me a story of her life in Austria when she was a young girl. It seems all she did was eat custard pudding and dance waltzes.

"I danced so, when I was first in love," she'd say.

Somehow I sense she didn't do those

waltzes with Grandpa but with someone else, a man she left there. Grandpa can't dance. And she gets misty eyed when she talks about it.

Nana's bedroom is blue and white. She's a regal lady with white hair who wears blue dresses and speaks with an Austrian accent. Grandpa speaks with a German accent and works as a cook in one of New York's fancy restaurants.

Sometimes he mumbles to himself in German.

Nana treats us special. She's the only grandmother I have. And the only thing I can't figure out is how she can be so nice and have such a miserable daughter.

CHAPTER

9

Before Nana and Grandpa arrived, however, Uncle Hermie came to visit us.

He's my father's older brother and the black sheep of the family. He isn't married, and he lives with a woman in an apartment in New York. This is not spoken of in polite company except in whispers, the way grown-ups speak when they think children's ears can't pick up the sound.

"He's a man-about-town, like Lamont Cranston," Martin explained to me and Tom. Lamont Cranston is The Shadow.

"But he's also a man of mystery," Martin added, "like Captain Midnight. Because the United States government doesn't know his identity."

"Why?" I asked.

"Because he wasn't born here, but in Italy. He has no papers, nothing's in his name, and he doesn't pay taxes."

"Why?" I asked again.

Martin shrugged. "Who knows? Maybe his job for the war effort is just too important."

The best part about Uncle Hermie is that he always smells of olives. This is because he manages a New York deli to cover up what he really does as a man of mystery. He drives a big black Buick, he always smiles, and he thinks my father is crazy for living in the country.

"What do you do here, watch the grass grow?" he always asks.

We children love him. He picks us up, cracks jokes, and gives us candies from the pockets of his pinstriped suits. And he has a secret password.

It's *Chicago*. Whenever we go out with him into a store or a restaurant, or if he's looking at something to buy and he doesn't like the looks of things, he says, "Chicago."

That means, "Let's get out of here." And everybody with him moves to leave.

You can't tell us children anything bad about Uncle Hermie. We won't believe it. My father always speaks of how, after their father died, Uncle Hermie quit school. Only, instead of going to work to help their mother support the younger ones, he hung around in pool halls.

We don't care about that. To us, he's wonderful because he has a password. There's a kind of magic and excitement about him when he pulls into our drive with his shiny black car and gets out in his pinstriped suit, wide tie, and fedora hat.

He's the only man-about-town that we know.

He brings the city with him. And we're fascinated with anything to do with the city. My father says there's evil in the city. People do terrible things there, and he moved us to the country so we could grow up clean.

On Palm Sunday, Uncle Hermie came to visit with his girlfriend Fanny. She's blond and looks like Marlene Dietrich in the movies.

My father loves all his brothers and sisters. But they don't come much. Amazing Grace doesn't like them. The reason for this is because they all remember my mother. There's a lot of tension when they come because we all know things could blow up any minute.

This Palm Sunday Uncle Hermie had candy for us. Because of the sugar shortage, we never get candy.

Except when I go to Mrs. Leudloff's. She'd given me candy again on my last visit. And again, I hadn't told anybody.

Fanny went into the kitchen to try to help Amazing Grace. I was getting a cup of coffee for Uncle Hermie when Fanny showed Amazing Grace a ring he had given her.

"That's beautiful." Amazing Grace turned to her, and she looked mad. "But I have a husband," she said.

Fanny sure is glamorous. She really did look like Marlene Dietrich that day. But she didn't know what to say to the remarks by Amazing Grace. I saw her face fall. And I felt bad for her.

After dinner, Uncle Hermie asked us children and my father to come outside with him. Out of the trunk of his car he took a large box.

"Stamp books," he said.

Sure enough, they were. Ration stamps, like you need to get food and shoes. All the things we need and never have enough of. They have pictures on them of guns and tanks and ships.

We kids call them coupons.

To me, they mean sugar. My small supply was gone now. I'd taken to eating Wheaties, the Breakfast of Champions, because they were better without sugar than Wheatena.

Now here was Uncle Hermie with a whole box of coupons! Where did he get them?

Martin, Tom, and I looked at each other. "Maybe he got them as a reward from the government," I heard Tom whisper.

Martin shook his head no.

"Go ahead, John," Uncle Hermie said to my father. "Take them. There are plenty more where these came from. You need them to feed your family."

My father looked confused for a moment.

"John," Uncle Hermie said in that soothing voice of his, "go ahead, take them."

"Don't, Daddy." Mary had come out of the house and was standing there wiping her hands on her apron. "They're black market."

Black market? It sounded like a new radio program, better than *Inner Sanctum*. I looked at Martin. He nodded at me. Martin knew. He'd tell me later.

"Mary," Uncle Hermie said, "you look like you need a new pair of shoes."

"I don't want shoes if it means not doing my best for the war effort," Mary said.

Yesterday she and Beverly had been to the theater in town to see *Mrs. Miniver*. It was all she talked about. Mrs. Miniver never cried, Mary told me this morning. She kept a stiff upper lip through the Nazi bombing of England.

Ever since she'd seen *Gone with the Wind*, Mary had wanted to be Scarlett O'Hara. Until yesterday. Now she wanted to be Greer Garson, who played Mrs. Miniver.

"War effort? A little kid like you?" Uncle Hermie laughed. "Aren't you doing enough? You're not seventeen yet and you're working in the arsenal. You never even finished high school."

"Neither did you," Mary snapped back.

He shrugged and smiled. "I left because I didn't want to stay. You left because your father made you."

"For the war effort," Mary said.

"For money," Uncle Hermie told her. "Because he wants the money you bring home. You lost the best part of your life, Mary. You don't need to give up any more."

"That's enough, Hermie," my father said angrily. "I'm doing my best to raise a family here. Do you know what that means?"

It was turning into a fight. This could easily happen when my father's family visited. Anything they said could trigger a fight. Because they remembered my mother. And they had loved her.

"Mary, take the coupons and buy yourself a pair of shoes," Uncle Hermie said again.

"We're fighting Hitler," Mary yelled at him. "We're fighting for freedom! Don't you know what that means?"

Uncle Hermie looked sad. "Mary," he said, "you've got no freedom in this house. I come here, and you kids are allowed to mention Hitler's name but not your dead mother's. Didn't you ever ask yourself why?"

Mary turned and ran into the house. "I don't ever want to see you again!" she yelled. She was crying. I knew she was Scarlett O'Hara then and not Mrs. Miniver. Because Mrs. Miniver never cried. And because Uncle Hermie laughed, just like Rhett Butler did when Scarlett threw the vase right after she declared her love for Ashley.

"Hermie, I think it's time for you to go," my father said.

"Ah, John."

"No, you'd better go now," my father said.

Uncle Hermie turned to us, me and Tom and Martin. "Want some coupons, kids? You look like you need shoes, too. You look like you need lots of things. How 'bout you, little Kay? You're the one who's always thinking. Never say anything, do you, kid? You know better."

And he knelt down in front of me. "You just keep your eyes and ears open, don't you? But you're always learning."

I was afraid to say anything. He liked me. All my father's family did. They all acted as if I was special to them. The feeling made me uncomfortable. And I try my best to be invisible when they come to visit. Because Amazing Grace will take it out on me later if they fuss over me too much.

"Here," and Uncle Hermie thrust some coupons into my hand. And into the hands of Martin, Tom, and Elizabeth. "Use them, kids. Don't believe that crap about winning the war effort by going without sugar, shoes, or meat. Kids have a right to such things. Kids have a right to their childhood."

All four of us took them, thanked him,

and hugged him. Then Fanny, who'd been standing in the background watching all this, came up to him and put her arm on his shoulder.

"Chicago, Hermie," she said.

He nodded.

"Good-bye, kids." Fanny winked at us and got into the shiny black Buick.

"Good-bye, John," he said to my father.

But my father didn't answer.

Uncle Hermie got into the car. "I'll be back, kids. I'm taking the boys to the Dodgers game Easter week. Be ready."

We stood watching them drive away. My father said nothing. Uncle Hermie, the man-about-town whose identity was so secret even the United States government didn't know he existed, would be back. And he would take my brothers to the Brooklyn Dodgers game. He did once every year.

"Can we keep the coupons, Daddy?" Tom asked.

"Sure." My father shrugged.

Later I asked Martin where he thought the coupons had come from.

"Black market," he said.

"You mean he isn't working for the war effort?"

"He's working for himself," Martin said.

I didn't care. Nobody spoke about the matter again. Mary acted like Mrs. Miniver for a week, but Tom and Martin chipped in from their allowance and bought me some sugar.

All that spring, every time I ate breakfast or had a cup of tea, I thanked Uncle Hermie for the coupons. I couldn't have gotten my new supply of sugar without them.

Later Martin told me what the black market was. People get the things they want, even though the war is on. Because dishonest men and crooked politicians make them pay higher prices for things they want. Or print counterfeit coupons and sell them to the people.

How Uncle Hermie came into all this, I didn't know. I didn't want to know. I loved him. He smelled of olives, was nice to us, and said kids should have a childhood.

And inside me I decided that he must be working for the war effort. He was probably with the FBI. And his job was so important that not even his superiors knew his identity.

I decided that this business with the coupons and the black market was just to keep that identity a secret. As for Fanny, well, she was his faithful sidekick. Like Margo Lane was to The Shadow. Like Tonto was to the Lone Ranger. And like Kato was to the Green Hornet.

CHAPTER

10

Our house was worse than *Suspense* that week. My father was upset because his brother had told us why Mary didn't finish high school. Amazing Grace was upset because of all the work that had to be done because her parents were coming.

She gave us all double duty. I had to polish the silver and wipe the dishes. Mary and Elizabeth not only took turns washing dishes at night but had to help do spring cleaning. I didn't mind drying because my sisters always sang when they washed.

Mary sang "I'll Walk Alone" and "I'll Be Seeing You" and "We'll Meet Again," the song Vera Lynn sang when she told us to keep smiling through.

Elizabeth sang "Rum and Coca-Cola" like the Andrews Sisters.

I thought they were both very good.

Tom had to put a new coat of whitewash on the inside of the barn. Martin had to rake all the flower beds. It was mid-April and everything outside needed doing.

In school Jennifer wouldn't come near me. She stayed with the Golden Band and let them lead her around by the nose. You'd have thought I was responsible for her brother's ship being torpedoed.

The only good thing that happened to me all week was that on Tuesday I won the toy from the new box of Kellogg's Pep. There's a toy in every box, and Martin, Tom, and I have figured out a way to decide which of us wins it.

Every morning my father listens to the news. My brothers and I each take a city. Mine is Rome, Tom's is Paris, and Martin's is London. Whoever has the city most mentioned on the news wins. Most mornings there's nothing to win. But that doesn't matter.

When we open a new box of Kellogg's Pep, there is. Rome won that day, and I pulled out a bombsight.

All the toys have to do with war. The bombsight came with a map of places in

Germany. Marbles came with it too, to drop as bombs.

"What cities will you bomb?" Tom asked.

"All the ones where the U-boats are made," I told him. "And I'll bomb the railroads they ship the torpedoes on."

The announcer said something on the radio about the Dionne quintuplets then. And we all listened.

"The five Dionnes, who will soon be ten years old, were in Superior, Wisconsin, yesterday to launch a new battleship," the announcer said in his deep voice. "The girls pulled straws to see who would smash the bottle. Emily won. And that was Niagara River water in the bottle, folks, not champagne."

"I wonder what they wore," Mary said.

"Probably those silly coats and hats and white stockings and Mary Janes," I said. "I hate those little girls."

"We don't hate in this house," my father said.

"They're your age, Kay," Martin reminded me.

I needed no reminding. Up in Canada the Dionnes are Superman, the Green Hornet, and The Shadow all rolled into one. And in the United States their pictures are wherever you look. On calendars, on magazine covers, in newsreels. Five little girls born to a poor farmer and his wife. And they *all* have Mary Janes.

"Never mind the Dionnes," Amazing Grace said. "Kay, here's egg money. You're to stop at Mrs. Leudloff's on your way home and get two dozen. We need them for Easter baking."

"Listen for the shortwave radio this time," Martin reminded me as we walked to get the school bus. "There are German spies all over the place. She's probably got a cache of rifles hidden in her cellar. Here, I'll give you my new magic pedometer, if you want it. It just came yesterday."

Did I *want* it? I couldn't wait to get my hands on it.

Martin strapped it on my wrist. "Be careful with it. It will protect you, as well as track any hidden rifles."

I said, "Gosh all hemlock," and thanked him twice. And about a dozen times that day I checked to make sure it was still on my wrist. Underneath the cuff of my long-sleeved uniform blouse. Where Sister Brigitta couldn't see it.

But the little dial on the pedometer didn't move at all when I got to Mrs. Leudloff's house.

I didn't expect it to move when Rex lunged and growled at me as I sneaked by his enclosure. Although it was magic, and I kind of hoped it would.

But the dial didn't even move when I walked right past Mrs. Leudloff's cellar windows, where I was sure the rifles were stored.

And the only radio I heard was the sound of *Lonely Women* drifting out from her kitchen window.

"Hello, you're back again. How nice." She had on a white blouse with red polka dots and a snappy bow at the neck. She wore slacks and a snood around her blond hair. She reminded me of the ad for Listerine antiseptic in Amazing Grace's *Ladies Home Journal*.

"Her secret can be yours," the ad said of the lovely lady who was smiling right through, with a smile as dazzling as her white blouse.

All the women in the ads had secrets about how to keep their teeth white, their gums from bleeding, their clothes young, and their pancakes light.

"I want two dozen today," I told Mrs. Leudloff. I followed her into the henhouse.

"And so? How did Tony and Marie work out?"

I said that they didn't.

"I told you, didn't I?" And she carefully placed the eggs in one carton. "So what will your mama do now?"

"Her parents are coming from the city."

"Ah, good to have parents. What's that you're wearing on your wrist?"

Mistake! She'd seen the pedometer! How could I have been so stupid! Jack Armstrong would never let anybody see it.

"It's a pedometer," I said weakly.

"Ah, like Jack Armstrong uses. Is that it?"

I stared at her in disbelief. *Does she know everything, this lady?*

"I listen to the radio," she explained. "Here all day alone, with my husband off to war, what else is there to do?"

Her husband off at war? For the Germans?

"I know all the songs, all the programs. I know how we women are supposed to be brave and save sugar, keep fit to do our jobs on the home front, stand behind our men in uniform, and keep smiling through."

Smiling through. How dare she say that? She's a German!

"And I know what you're looking for with that pedometer, too. A cache of rifles." And she laughed and put her hands on her hips. "You think I'm a German spy? You believe what the children in the neighborhood say about me?"

I wanted to die. I felt myself blushing. I wished the ground would open up and swallow me. But then I remembered that sometimes spies fool people by being open and honest.

"No, ma'am," I said.

"Do I look like a spy?"

"No. You look like Greta Garbo."

"Good. We can't have any of that nonsense between us. We're friends, aren't we?"

"Yes."

"Now, what kind of candy do you prefer? Caramels or gumdrops?"

"Caramels."

She reached into her slacks pocket and pulled out a handful of caramels and dropped them into my hand.

I thanked her, still embarrassed.

She was smiling down at me. "I like listening to Mrs. Roosevelt on the radio best. And I listen to *Lights Out*. Do you?"

"Oh, yes!"

"They're going to do a rebroadcast of 'Chicken Heart.' Did you ever listen to that one?"

"Yes. The heart grows and grows and thumps and thumps, until it consumes the whole world."

We laughed together. "But it scares me," I confided.

She patted my shoulder. "You shouldn't be scared. It's just a story. Don't be scared of stories. Or rumors. We worry about all the wrong things in life. And what really can harm us we never worry about. Do you know why?"

"Why?"

"Because we aren't smart enough to worry about what will really harm us. If we were, we'd be fortune-tellers and make lots of money. Go now, and don't worry. You're too serious for such a little girl."

I went, eating my caramels. I felt twice as guilty this visit. Not only had I accepted her candy again, but I liked her. She was a nice lady. She knew how to talk to me.

I could never tell anyone at home that. They'd think I was crazy.

But worse, by being friends with her, I'd

relaxed my efforts to help speed victory. "You must never relax, but keep on punching," Glenn Riggs the announcer told us on the radio.

I'd let him down. I'd let my brothers down. I'd let Jen down. And her brother, who'd been torpedoed. Jen must have known I was a weak-kneed, loose-lipped fool. No wonder she didn't want any more to do with me.

CHAPTER

11

"Kay," Nana said to me, "come thread this needle. My eyes are old."

She was sitting in an Adirondack chair out on the lawn on Easter Saturday. She and Grandpa had met my father in New York on Friday night and come home with him on the train.

How could anybody's eyes be so old they couldn't thread a needle? I put Mary Frances down and threaded it for Nana.

She was making Mary Frances a new dress for Easter. Nobody had ever thought to make Mary Frances a dress. I was delighted, of course. What with the war and everything, Mary Frances's wardrobe had been neglected worse than mine. And the dress wasn't of feed-bag material, either. It was from some scraps of blue dimity.

"After this I will make something for the new baby," Nana said.

"What?"

"A little dress."

"What if it's a boy? They don't wear dresses."

"They do when they are babies. You must be a help to your mother now, you know, with this baby coming."

I said yes, I would be.

"It will be nice, having a baby in the family. You'll enjoy that," she said.

I hadn't thought much about the baby as a real person. So far it was only an excuse for Amazing Grace to get everybody to wait on her hand and foot.

A baby in the house? That would be exciting. I must get used to the idea. "Where will they put it?" I asked.

"In your mama's room in the beginning."

"Then in mine," I said dismally. "I'll have to give up my room and stay with my sisters."

"Do you mind being with them now?" She put down her needle and looked at me over her glasses.

"No," I said. Their room is very large, with three windows. My bed had been put in one corner. And I liked it because when they weren't around, I could snoop in their things. Mary had a large chimney closet next to her bed that I could crawl into. It was full of magazines about Shirley Temple. Elizabeth had magazines on Loretta Young.

"But the baby should be a boy," I told Nana. "Boys have it better in the world."

"Now, that's not true, Kay."

"Yes, it is. Look at Tom and Martin. This week Daddy's taking them to New York with him so Uncle Hermie can take them to see the Brooklyn Dodgers play. And they're staying with Uncle Hermie overnight, too."

She shrugged. "Who wants to see the Brooklyn Dodgers play?"

"I do. I want to see Pee Wee Reese and Pete Reiser."

"Well, maybe Grandpa can take you somewhere when they go. Grandpa?" she called to him.

"Ya, Mama, what is it?"

He was repainting the top half of my father's car lights with black paint. All car lights have to be blacked out on top. So we can't be seen by submarines lurking offshore. Or by any German or Jap planes not spotted by our air-raid wardens.

The paint on our car lights was two years old and peeling.

"Grandpa, maybe this week when the boys go to the ball game, you could take Kay somewhere? You could drive John to the station in the morning and keep the car and take her to town."

"I'll take her somewhere, sure," he said. "But I don't need the car."

"Then where would you take her?" Nana was sewing, then she dropped her needle in her lap. "No, Grandpa, you will *not* go to Ernie's!"

"Mama, if I want to go to Ernie's, I'll go," he said.

"No, Grandpa. Do not go. There is trouble."

"What trouble, Mama?" he asked. "You see trouble behind every bush. Ernie is my friend. If I want to go see him, I'll go. I'll get Kay some ice cream. What's the harm in getting a little girl some ice cream?"

On Easter Monday, Tom and Martin got all their chores done so they could go to New York the next day.

One of Martin's chores is collecting the tin cans and newspapers for the scrap drive. I usually help him with the tin cans.

First we peel the paper off the cans. Then I stand at one end of the kitchen and Martin stands at the other. We make a game of it.

He rolls the can to me. And just as it gets to my feet, I jump and stamp on it to flatten it.

We rolled and flattened several cans, and Martin was putting them in a box when he looked at me.

"I'm taking them to the salvage bin in the wagon this afternoon," he said. "I've always had the biggest haul of scrap. But do you know what they need most?"

"No," I said.

"Rubber. They need lots of rubber to fight the war. Do you want to give us your rubber baby doll?"

I stared down at him hard. "Are you crazy? *Give Mary Frances?* I can't do that."

"Why?"

"Why?" For a minute I couldn't think why. Then I did. "Because they'd tear her apart and kill her. She can't die."

"Why?"

Why? Didn't boys understand anything? They all wanted to be Superman and bend steel with their bare hands and change the course of mighty rivers. But they didn't understand why a girl couldn't give her one and only baby doll to the scrap drive.

Because Mary Frances is more than a baby doll, that's why. She's my friend. I hug her at night, when I'm afraid. Or when I've been hit by Amazing Grace or yelled at by my father.

"Because Nana just made her a new dress," I said. "And you can't die when you've just been given a new dress."

To give Martin credit, he didn't argue. "Okay," he said. I thought that was very decent of him.

On Easter Tuesday morning Tom and Martin got up extra early and dressed in their good spring knickers, polished shoes, high socks, dress shirts, ties, jackets, and peaked caps, and with their overnight bags, went with my father to get the train for New York.

The house was very quiet. Mary and Elizabeth had gone off to work. Nana and Amazing Grace were still sleeping.

Grandpa was up, and I made his breakfast. First he had his orange, then one egg, some toast, and black coffee.

I sat waiting to put the egg in the boiling water. It must be boiled no longer than three minutes. He is very exact about everything. Mary Frances sat on a chair next to me in her new dress.

I watched him eat his orange. First he peels it, then takes it apart carefully and eats one piece at a time. But that isn't the interesting part.

The interesting part is the way he mumbles to himself while he eats it. He carries on a whole conversation with himself. Never mind that I am right there in the room.

He seems to be arguing with somebody over something. And it is the same argument every morning. Finally now, however, he finished, and looked at me and smiled.

"Is it time to put the eggs in the water?" I asked. I was going to have an egg, too.

"Ya, put them in."

I did so. Then I put the toast in the toaster and sat back down. He timed the eggs in his head. He knew when the three minutes were up.

"That's a nice dolly you've got there," he said while we were waiting.

Mary Frances was considerably more than a dolly, but I said thank you just the same.

"What's her name?"

"Mary Frances."

"That's a long name."

"It was supposed to be mine," I said.

He scowled.

So I told him then how my mother had a long name picked out for me. And I didn't know what it was. But I decided it should have been Mary Frances.

"That name doesn't suit you," he said.

"But I'd be a better person with such a name."

"What's wrong with how you are now?"

I shrugged. Everything was wrong with me. Couldn't he see that? "I'd like to be like Betty Fairfield on the *Jack Armstrong* program. She's always having adventures. And her father takes her everywhere with her brother, Billy, and her cousin Jack. I always have to stay home."

He listened with great interest. "I thought you wanted to be a tap dancer. Like Shirley Temple."

I blushed. Mary must have told him this. I'd confided it to her the day she'd bought me the Mary Janes. But since all the trouble with the Mary Janes, all the bad feeling, and since we'd had to return them, I was turned against tap dancing.

I decided I'd much rather be Betty Fairfield,

who wore a luminous bracelet and went around the world on jaunts with her father, who never scolded and only spoke up when important decisions had to be made.

"This afternoon I'll take you for ice cream," Grandpa said. "Don't you want ice cream?"

"Yes," I said politely. But how could I tell him that Betty went in the *Silver Albatross,* her kindly father's hydroplane, to places like Africa or the Andes?

I couldn't even go with my brothers to see the Brooklyn Dodgers play.

CHAPTER

12

It was a warm April. By afternoon the sun was actually hot. I felt its warmth on my back as I followed Grandpa on the path through the fields in back of our house. It was a long walk, but I didn't mind. I felt like Betty Fairfield, hacking through the jungles of the Philippines.

Nana had been napping when we left. She and Grandpa had argued once again about his taking me to Ernie's.

"Don't go, Grandpa, please," she'd begged. There was fear in her voice. "Bad things will happen."

"Bah," he told her. "Be quiet. You're getting old, woman."

So Nana got quiet and went to her room to nap.

Amazing Grace was sewing my feed-bag dress on her Singer.

Why didn't Nana want him to go? What bad thing could happen on a sun-filled day in the country? Maybe Nana was listening to too many radio programs, I thought. She liked her radio, too.

Her favorite was *The Adventures of the Thin Man*. Nick and Nora Charles were the happiest, merriest married couple in radio. Nick was a private eye who was always coming upon dead bodies.

Did Nana think we'd come upon dead bodies in the fields behind our house? All we came upon were chirping birds, droning bees, and a sun that seemed to have stopped in its tracks as we walked along the path that mid-April afternoon.

Well, if we came on a dead body, I'd know what to do, all right. I'd act just like Betty and track down the criminals before they got away. No, I didn't have a luminous bracelet, but Martin had given me his magic pedometer again that morning. I guess he felt sorry for me because I couldn't go to Brooklyn.

I got my ice cream. Strawberry. Two scoops.

Ernie's is a pretty place. It's a roadside stand where you can get good sandwiches, root beer, the real kind of beer for grown-ups, and ice cream. It has a small lake out back where there are picnic tables.

Grandpa set my ice cream down on a picnic table and told me he was going to talk to his friend. "Will you be all right?"

How could I not be all right? It was a sunny day, I had just been bought ice cream, and there were ducks on the lake, and a couple of picnicking families at other tables.

Better yet, Amazing Grace was nowhere in sight to tell me I wasn't holding my spoon right or I was eating too fast. I was in heaven. "Yes," I said.

He went off to see his friend, and I ate my ice cream. I took my time finishing it, walked down to the lake, watched the ducks for a while, and walked back to my table again.

Grandpa had been gone an awful long time. I decided to go and see if he was okay.

I came around to the side of Ernie's just in time to hear Grandpa talking through the little window where you give your order.

"So how is he doing, then?" he was asking. "Is he making a new Germany?"

I couldn't see Ernie's face on the other

side of the window, but I could hear his voice.

"He is trying, but it isn't easy, with the war. My friend Hauptmann writes that our people back there are suffering. Not enough to eat. They work long, hard hours, and the Americans are bombing the factories."

"Hauptmann?" Grandpa asked.

"Ya," the voice from behind the window said. "He used to be a professor at Rutgers. He is now back in the Fatherland, in charge of cultural interests for the Third Reich."

Grandpa said something then, but I did not hear it. All I heard was a buzzing in my ears and the pounding of my own heart.

They are talking about Hitler. And Germany, I thought.

They are talking about how the German people are suffering! And a man named Hauptmann, who does something for the Third Reich!

Grandpa cares about these people? He asked how Hitler was doing with his new Germany! How can he care?

The sun felt so hot on my head! My palms were sweating. My knees were weak.

How can they be talking about such things, right here at Ernie's where strawberry ice cream is served to people and there are ducks swimming in the lake?

"Hauptmann has sent me pamphlets," the voice behind the window went on. "They tell of the wonders of the new Germany. He wants me to distribute them. Will you take some back to Brooklyn?"

"Let me see one," Grandpa said.

A paper was shoved through the window. Grandpa took it and looked at it briefly.

All I could think of for one terrible moment was, *I'm behind enemy lines. I must do something.*

But what?

I tried to speak. I wanted to scream out, "No, don't take it," like Mary did when Uncle Hermie offered the coupons to my father. But just as I was about to do so, there came a squeal of brakes as a car pulled up in front and raised dust on the gravel.

At the same time, Grandpa folded the paper, then turned, saw me standing there, and scowled. "What are you doing here? Didn't I tell you to stay at the table?"

"Yes."

"Then what are you doing here? Can't you obey?"

He was angry. But before his anger could

grow, some tough-looking men in city suits and ties and fedora hats came up behind him. "Out of the way, old man. We want to talk with Ernie here."

Grandpa stood aside.

They went up to the window. "So, this is the Nazi hideaway in New Jersey, is it?" they taunted. "Are you Ernie?"

The voice from behind the window said yes. "But I'm no Nazi."

"That's not what we hear," one of the three men said. They looked like G-men from *Gang Busters,* which comes on Friday nights, sponsored by Sloan's Liniment. Their tires had screeched just like on the show. But they had no machine guns.

"We hear you have Bund rallies here," one of the men said.

"No Bund rallies," came the voice from behind the window.

"No? We hear you kicked a man out of here last week because he was wearing the uniform of a United States soldier."

"He was drunk," the voice behind the window said. "This is a family place."

"Family place, is it? I'll just bet," said another of the three men. "Picnicking, beer drinking, marching. A German boot camp, is what we hear. Do you have uniformed camp police and kids like Hitler's youth in brown shirts?"

At that moment Grandpa turned to me. "Kay, go back to the picnic table."

But I just stood there frozen. You didn't run when you were behind enemy lines or fighting evil. Did Jack Armstrong and Betty run when they were trapped in the Cave of the Mummies?

"Kay! Go. Now! What's the matter with you?"

When Grandpa was upset or angry, his German accent became stronger. So he didn't say "What's the matter with you?" He said, "Vat's the matter mit you?"

Mistake.

The three men turned to look at him. "You a Hitler lover too, mister?"

Grandpa stood his ground. He didn't back off. "No, no," he said, only it came out, *"Nein, nein."*

If that wasn't enough, the paper in Grandpa's hand was. "What's this?" one of the men grabbed it, read it quickly. "Look at this, boys," he said to his companions. "Nazi propaganda."

One of them grabbed Grandpa roughly by

the sleeve. "What do you two have going here?" they demanded. "A Hitler rally? Don't you know New Jersey passed an anti-Nazi law nine years ago?"

Grandpa's face got red. He tried to pull away. "Leave me be," he said. He started to struggle.

Fear gripped me. It overcame me like nothing I had ever known before.

The man who was holding Grandpa shook him roughly.

"No!" I screamed.

Before I could do anything else, they pushed him to the ground. He went down, hard. I heard the smack of his head as it hit the ground. Heard him say "Oof" as the breath went out of him.

"Grandpa!" I ran to him.

Some women from the picnic tables out back came to see what was going on, saw him go down, and screamed. "Who are you people?" one woman asked the three men. "How dare you come here and rough up the patrons! Elsie, call the police!"

"We're leaving, lady," one of the men said.

The woman named Elsie was at the outside phone already. Ernie was shutting his little window. The three men started to leave. Before they did one of them picked up a stone and threw it at the window.

Glass shattered. Two other women screamed. Some men came running from the picnic tables. A child with one of the women started to cry.

I'd heard glass shatter on *Gang Busters*. The program starts with a window breaking, a police siren, a burglar alarm going off, and then machine guns firing and tires screeching.

But the sound of this broken glass, together with that child crying and the women screaming, was like nothing I had ever heard before in my life.

I knelt beside Grandpa. The side of his head was bleeding. I didn't know what to do. "Grandpa," I cried. "Grandpa."

"The police are coming," the woman by the phone said.

The three men had stood as if frozen, too, by the whole crazy scene. At the word "police" they ran to their car with the New York plates. So I knew they weren't G-men.

They got into the car, fast. I got up and ran over to the front of the building. Just before they pulled away I saw the license plate.

735-RU-6.

I sealed the number in my head, the way Betty Fairfield would do. Then I went back to Grandpa as the car careened away, raising dust on the gravel.

By now Grandpa was sitting up. Ernie was standing over him. One of the women had a towel and ice. Two men customers helped him to his feet and another brought over a chair. They sat him down.

"Let me do it," I said to Ernie as he was about to put the ice, wrapped in a towel, on Grandpa's head. I was shaking.

"Hold the ice on his head, there's a good girl," a woman said to me. I did so. I just sat there holding that ice up to his head while he kept saying he was fine and the other customers stood around talking about hoodlums and hecklers and how they didn't know what the world was coming to.

I was still sitting there holding the ice on his head when the police arrived.

"Go home, Kay," Grandpa said.

"I want to stay with you."

I stayed while the police questioned Ernie. They knew him. "The same crowd as last time?" one officer asked Ernie.

He said yes. "I'm getting sick and tired of

it. A man can't make a decent living anymore without being accused of being a Nazi."

It was then that I saw the pamphlet on the ground behind Grandpa's chair. I got up while everyone was watching the police, and I picked the pamphlet up and put it in my dress pocket.

The police came over to Grandpa. They asked him his name and what had started the trouble. They asked if he could identify any of the men or the car.

"I have the license-plate number," I told them.

They smiled down at me. "Smart little girl," one said. "What is it?"

I gave it to them.

Grandpa just sat there, dazed. He didn't say anything, except that he didn't want any trouble. No, he didn't want to press charges. He just wanted to go home.

"I'm afraid we can't let you do that, mister," one of the officers said. "That head doesn't look so good. I'm afraid we're going to have to take you to the hospital for a look-see."

The way they said "look-see" was real nice. Like Uncle Jim would say it on *Jack Armstrong*.

"And then we'll want to question you," the officer said.

I got scared then. The police were going to take Grandpa.

"Kay"—Grandpa stood up—"go on home."

"I want to go with you."

"Go home," he said. "I'm all right. I'm fine. Go home and tell Nana I'm good. And I'll be home later."

I stood watching him get into the police car. Then I ran across the highway, up the hill, and down the path to home.

I ran all the way, my breath coming in spurts, my braids flapping, branches from bushes slapping my face. By the time I burst in the back door, I had such a pain in my side I could hardly talk.

Nana was at the kitchen table cleaning string beans.

"Kay," she said. "What's the matter, child?"

Amazing Grace came into the room. "How many times have I told you not to slam that back door—," she started. Then she stopped, seeing me. "What happened?"

"Grandpa," I said. "He's been taken."

CHAPTER

13

Our house was in such an uproar that night, nobody even thought to tune in to any radio program. Amazing Grace took to her bed. My father came home and had to milk the cow himself because Grandpa couldn't do it and Tom and Martin were in the city.

The police brought Grandpa home just as my father was coming in the door. He spoke with them.

Nana stood white-faced in the kitchen, her hands folded across her stomach. "Well, Grandpa, and what did I tell you?" was the first thing she said.

He mumbled something that sounded like "Oh, Mama, go tell yourself," refused to eat supper, and went to lie down.

My father called me into his library. It has

a lot of bookcases, french doors that over-look the garden, a wood stove, and his desk. The books are all for grown-ups, except for the encyclopedias and a copy of *The Water Babies,* which I love to look at.

"Kay, what happened?" my father asked.

When my father asked "what happened" in any other part of the house, it wasn't so bad. When he called me into his library to ask it, it was serious.

For a moment I just stood there. I looked at the picture of Amazing Grace on his desk. And I wondered, for the hundredth time, what harm it would have done if he'd had a picture of my mother somewhere in the house. Not on his desk, no. But maybe in a little corner someplace, behind a hanging plant.

I don't even know what my mother looked like.

There are times I hate my father for that. Did he love my mother? If I thought he still did, I could probably forgive him for not having pictures around. But I thought he didn't. I thought that Amazing Grace had clouded his mind.

I told him the same thing I'd told Amazing Grace and Nana. I did not tell him about the pamphlet, or about how Grandpa and Ernie were talking about Hitler.

"Grandpa was talking to Ernie and some men came and made trouble and Grandpa got in their way," I said.

"Just make sure this doesn't upset your mother," he said. "We can't have her upset now." He turned to the mail on his desk.

That was all. He didn't care about me. I left, glad I hadn't told him about the pamphlet.

In my sisters' room that night, I looked at the pamphlet for the first time. I used my flashlight. Mary Frances sat next to me. I couldn't believe what I was reading.

"We Germans in America are living together on a small island in a hostile ocean," it said. "Contact with the enemy should be made only through the captain of your group."

It went on to say there are fifteen million people of German blood in America. And they have to keep their racial identity pure.

It said the Jews are inferior. It said the Germans in America should spread the word about German culture. And it said disobedience is treachery.

I didn't understand a lot of it. But I was

glad Elizabeth and Mary were still downstairs. I sensed the pamphlet was everything that the war was all about, that it was a dangerous piece of paper. And that not even Betty Fairfield would know what to do about it.

I needed powers and abilities far beyond those of mortal men, like Superman's, to know what was to be done with it.

I did nothing.

I hid the pamphlet under my pillow that night. The next day I kept it in the pocket of my jeans. I must have felt to see if it was there a hundred times. It burned against my hip. I walked around in a daze all that day.

In the afternoon the reporter called from the *Waterville Times*.

Amazing Grace spoke to him. "Interview the little girl who gave the police the license-plate number?" she asked him on the phone. "I think not. We don't want any publicity about this."

I was sweeping off the front stoop. The phone was in the center hall. I saw her shadow on the Persian carpet runner.

That reporter must have been real good. Like Lois Lane on *The Adventures of Superman*. Or maybe they had a crabby editor at the *Waterville Times*, like Perry White.

Because Amazing Grace gave in. "Well, all right," she said. "When do you want to come? Tomorrow? A photographer? You want to bring a photographer? Well, she's a very plain, uninteresting little girl, you know. I don't see what all the fuss is about." And then she laughed. "Well, if you want *me* in the picture with her, I suppose it could be arranged. I am her mother, after all."

She put the phone down, opened the front door, and stood looking down at me. "Now see what you've done? Brought attention down on us. You know your father doesn't like attention. We're quiet people, good people. Why did you have to give them the license-plate number?"

I said I didn't know. I said they'd asked me. And I thought it was right to do.

She set me to hoeing the garden that afternoon. The garden had to be ready for spring planting. I hoed for two hours. I got blisters on my hands, and I missed my afternoon radio programs.

Nana felt sorry for me when I came in out of the heat. She put ointment on my hands and gave me cold milk and put some Bosco in it.

"Ssh," she said, putting her finger to her

lips. "We don't have to tell your mama. Take it outside."

I took my cold milk with Bosco and sat outside under the sticker tree. Martin and Tom would be home soon with my father.

What would I do? Could I tell them about the pamphlet? Never mind them, what would I tell the reporters when they came?

Would I be brave and speak up for truth, justice, and the American way? Like Superman? Would I keep on punching for victory? Like Hop Harrigan?

Could I have no mercy for those who stepped over the line? Like Lamont Cranston, The Shadow?

Could I help track down public enemies who were trying to destroy America? Like the Green Hornet?

Could I just be brave, like Betty Fairfield?

I knew what was right to do. But I didn't know if I could do it. I needed a kindly Uncle Jim to advise me. I wandered about the house listlessly after supper. Grandpa had stayed in bed all day. He was up now, eating supper alone in the kitchen. His head was still bandaged. Nana sat across from him.

"Kay," Nana said. "When those men come from the newspaper tomorrow, you speak good of Grandpa, yes? He won't be here to speak for himself."

I looked into her wrinkled, kind face. "Where is he going?"

"Back to Brooklyn. Tomorrow morning."

I didn't have to ask why.

"Leave the child be, Mama," he said to her.

"I just want to tell her to speak good of you."

"She speaks what she knows. Right, Kay?"

I looked at him. He didn't know what I'd heard. Or that I had the pamphlet. I nodded yes and ran from the room.

I ran across the fields, down to my favorite part of the brook, where a narrow stone ledge jutted out over the water. I lay face down on the ledge, dangling Mary Frances over the clear bubbling water. I could see small fish in the brook below.

I heard rushing footsteps behind me. My brothers. They were home.

"You've had an adventure," Martin said.

I nodded yes.

"How does it feel?"

I shrugged and sat on the ledge, holding Mary Frances in my lap.

"We went to the ball game." Tom complained, "The Dodgers lost."

"They always lose," I said. "That's why people call them the Bums."

"We know that," Martin argued. "The point is, you stayed home and had all the fun."

"It wasn't fun," I told them.

"And now, tomorrow, reporters will come," Tom went on, "and you'll talk to them. You'll be in the newspaper."

"Amazing Grace will do all the talking," I said.

"She wasn't there," Martin reminded me. "You were. What are you going to say?"

I shrugged. "What's the Bund?" I asked Martin.

He told me. "It's the American Nazi party. They're strong in New Jersey. Why?"

I looked into the faces of my two brothers. For all they knew, they really knew nothing, I decided.

I was that way yesterday. I wished I could still be that way today.

"Those men who hit Grandpa said the Bund met at Ernie's."

Martin nodded and eyed me knowingly.

"So close to home," I pushed. "Do you think it's possible?"

"It's possible," Martin said.

"Wow," Tom murmured.

We sat in silence for a while. The only sounds were the bubbling of the brook and the chirping of birds. And then I thought to ask, "How's Uncle Hermie and Fanny?"

"They took us to supper at a Chinese restaurant," Martin said. "And he let us stay up late to listen to the radio."

I'd never had Chinese food. Once a year when Amazing Grace took us into New York and my father met us for supper, we went to The Reef, a fish house with sawdust on the floor. I hate fish.

"I wonder if the reporter who comes tomorrow will be mild mannered, like Clark Kent?" Tom asked.

Clark Kent is really Superman, only nobody knows it. Not even Lois Lane. She loves Superman, and she always makes fun of Clark.

I thought how wonderful it would be to have another identity. To be able to go into a broom closet and rip off your clothes and come out in a tight-fitting outfit with a cape and fly out of a window. And leave all the people who were mean to you standing there, gaping up.

"I don't know what the reporter will be like," I said.

There was nothing else to say then, so we all turned to go back to the house.

I started to take the pedometer off my wrist. "Here," I said to Martin, "you better take it back."

He waved me off. "You keep it for now," he said. "You'll need it tomorrow when you talk to the reporter."

CHAPTER

14

I awoke the next morning with a feeling of doom. For a moment I couldn't think why. Then I heard Nana calling me to come and have breakfast, so I dressed quickly and went downstairs.

I'd overslept. My father had already left for work, taking Grandpa with him to the train. Martin was outside doing chores. Tom was milking the cow, and Elizabeth and Mary were rushing about getting ready to leave, too.

I stood on the bottom step in the hall, blinking.

"Kay, come have your oatmeal," Nana called from the kitchen.

My sisters were putting on lipstick, and Mary was fussing with the high pompadour on top of her head. The folded smocks that the girls wore over their clothes at work were on a chair.

Mary came and grabbed me and pulled me into the middle of the hall, so I couldn't be seen from the kitchen. "You be careful what you say to that reporter today," she whispered. "Don't say anything against Grandpa. Or you'll upset Mother."

Elizabeth only scowled, and then when Mary went into the kitchen, she drew me aside. "You say what you have to say," she whispered. And then she gathered up her things and left.

I stood watching her go. Somehow I wasn't surprised. Amazing Grace is at her meanest when it comes to Elizabeth. She gives her all the worst chores and blames her for everything. Once when Elizabeth talked back to her, my father made Elizabeth kneel at our stepmother's feet and say she was sorry.

I never will forget how Elizabeth cried while she knelt. And I think Elizabeth will never forget it, either.

I went into the kitchen to have breakfast. "I wanted to have your feed-bag dress done today for when the reporter comes," Amazing Grace said. "I wanted to show him how we work in this house for the war effort. But I haven't finished it yet."

Well, I thought, *there's one good thing about today, anyway.*

"So you'll wear your white organdy that you wear to church on Sunday."

White organdy! In front of a reporter! That was ridiculous. Reporters hung around newsrooms where women like Lois Lane dressed in suits and polka-dot blouses with spiffy bows at the neck.

"Can't I just wear my dungarees?" I asked. "The organdy is so dressy."

"You'll wear what I say!" she snapped. "And you'll not answer any questions of his until I nod and tell you to do so."

"Grace," Nana said, "don't talk so to the child."

"Mind your business, Mother. You don't know what I have to put up with around here all the time." Amazing Grace turned her attention again to me. "And take that stupid thing off your wrist when the reporter comes."

I gasped. "It's my pedometer. I need it!"

"It's nonsense. Where did you get it?"

"It's Martin's. He loaned it to me. It's magic! I can't take it off!"

"You'll do as I say if you know what's

good for you. Now take that money on the counter there and go to Mrs. Leudloff's. We need eggs," Amazing Grace said. "You have time. The reporter doesn't come until ten-thirty."

I didn't have time and Amazing Grace knew it. She was up to one of her tricks. She has a lot of them.

One is that if she thinks I'm looking forward to some event, she'll find last-minute things to keep me busy. So I end up being late.

Once when she and my father were to take me to school in the evening to be in a play, she kept me so busy with last-minute chores that I didn't have time to dress right. Or even comb my hair. Then I got so nervous, I threw up when I got to school.

I've learned never to let her know that I'm looking forward to anything. Or she'll set out to ruin it for me.

I guess she thought I was looking forward to the reporter coming. If she only knew how much I dreaded it, she wouldn't have bothered sending me to Mrs. Leudloff's.

By the time I got out of the house it was ten. It was a good fifteen-minute walk each way. I hurried, because if I didn't, Amazing Grace would do the talking to the reporter. And I didn't know what kind of lies she would tell him about me. She'd already told him I was plain and uninteresting.

I knew I was plain. But I didn't think I was uninteresting.

So I nearly ran all the way.

I wished I could keep right on running, too, right past Mrs. Leudloff's house, right to the corner where we get the school bus. Only I wished then I could get the regular bus that went to Waterville. And just stay on it for as far as it went and never come home.

Because I still didn't know what I was going to tell that reporter. The pamphlet was still in my pocket. I'd slept, again, with it under my pillow.

I fell once. I went down on my knee and hurt it bad, right through the dungarees. I was limping and the breath was out of me by the time I got to Mrs. Leudloff's gate.

I opened it carefully. Just when I did that, I noticed that the latch was down on Rex's enclosure.

Rex's gate was open, only he didn't know it.

He was sleeping. Laid out flat and snoozing in the sun. He hadn't heard me approaching. I figured it was because I never came this time of day. Nobody did. People came after work or after school.

Rex was caught off guard.

I stayed outside the gate and looked around for Mrs. Leudloff. She was nowhere in sight. There was no radio playing. The place was as silent as the Cave of the Mummies.

If I called out to her, Rex would hear me and come to life. If she was home, that was all right. But what if she wasn't home?

I had to get the eggs. And get back home to be there in time for the reporter.

I remembered my first visit, when Mrs. Leudloff told me to walk right into the henhouse and take the eggs I needed and leave money. Because she trusted me.

I can't wait around forever, I decided. *I'm late now. And my knee is throbbing. I won't be able to run much on the way home.*

If only I could cloud minds. Like The Shadow. *How does he do it?* I wondered as I opened the gate softly. *What trick did he learn in the Orient? If I try real hard, can I do it, too?*

Can you cloud dogs' minds? Sister Brigitta said animals have no souls. *Doesn't that mean their minds are weak?*

I took a deep breath. *I'll just have to count on the magic pedometer to plot my way to the henhouse,* I decided.

I made my way across the soft grass in the yard, toward the far fence, where the daffodils bloomed, bright and yellow. I held my breath and made no sound.

I was almost to the henhouse. There was a door at my end. *I'll open it quietly,* I thought, *get inside, and close it fast.*

I had one foot raised and was just about to put it back down when I heard the growl. It was low and threatening.

It was the worst sound I'd heard in my life.

It was even worse than the breaking glass at Ernie's.

I stood there, frozen. Rex was sitting up, looking at me. He was curling back his lips, and soon his fangs would be dripping.

I stood very still, one foot still raised.

Rex got to his feet. But it wasn't like he was just standing up. He *lunged,* growling at the same time. It was all done together, the lunging and the growling.

He came at me. Faster than a speeding bullet. More powerful than a locomotive. He came at me like Superdog.

I screamed and put one arm over my face. I could *hear* him coming at me. He made a whooshing sound.

I screamed again and sank onto the ground.

I'm going to die here, I thought. *In Mrs. Leudloff's yard. I'm going to be ripped to pieces by her Nazi dog.* I waited for the first bite, praying I could be as strong as the martyrs Sister Brigitta told us about, who stood and let those Roman lions eat them rather than renounce their Christian faith.

"Rex!"

I heard a door slam. Heard her voice. But I *felt* Rex. He was standing over me. I felt his hot breath right over my face. I looked up.

He was standing over me, fangs dripping, ready to attack when he got the word. I saw his long red tongue, his sharp, pointy teeth, his glittering eyes.

"Rex! *Nein! Nein!*"

I heard her words, sharp and clear. Orders. Rex heard them, too. He sat.

She came rushing down the steps and across the yard. *"Nein, nein.* Sit!"

He sat. He cowered under her words. He whined.

"Go back to your house. *Raus mit* you!"

He turned and went to sit back down near his enclosure.

"Child, child, I am so sorry. I did not know you were here. What are you doing here this time of day?"

I looked up at her. I saw her shining bobbed hair, her spiffy blouse, her red fingernails. For a moment I couldn't speak. My voice was gone. She was smiling down at me. She had her arms outstretched.

I found my voice, finally. And when I did speak it came pouring out, all of it. All about the Christians and the lions, my hurt knee, how I was going to be late for the reporter, how I tried to cloud Rex's mind, and how the magic pedometer saved me.

Next thing I knew she was hugging me and patting me and I was bawling like a stuck pig. After that, she was leading me, still bawling, up the steps and into her house.

CHAPTER

15

"This isn't *my* Germany," Mrs. Leudloff said.

We sat at her kitchen table. In her hand she held the pamphlet. She was reading it.

"No, no." And she shook her head so that her shining bobbed hair shook, too. "This is not the Germany I know. Hitler is not Germany. He is not a leader. He is a madman."

I sipped my soda and took a bite of a homemade sugar cookie. She'd washed my face and bandaged my knee. She'd made me sit, and she'd listened as I poured out my story to her. And my worries about what I would say to the reporter.

Never did I think I could talk to her like this. Or to anyone. I think what made me do it was that she listened.

Nobody ever listens to me in school or at

home. Nobody cares what I think or fear. It was a new feeling, being listened to, and I liked it.

When I protested that I couldn't stay, that I had to get home, she waved away my objections. "I'll drive you home in a few minutes," she said.

"But the reporter . . ."

"He'll wait a few minutes. He came to see you, not your mama."

So I stayed.

"I have people at home, in Germany," she told me. "They are not happy with Hitler. My husband fights in the army of this country. We have a good life here. He made the difficult choice to fight against his homeland. We all must make hard choices these days. And so you, too, must make a choice. To do what is right and show this pamphlet to the reporter."

"Yes," I said. And I took another sip of soda. "But what trouble will it cause at home?"

"You did not make the trouble. You only ran into it."

"But Amazing Grace will be upset. My father said I shouldn't upset her."

"Upset? Child, the whole world is upset.

People are being gassed, put in prisons, starved, tortured. Soldiers are dying every day. *This* is being upset."

"Yes," I said again, "but what about Grandpa?"

"What about him?"

"I don't think he knew what was in the pamphlet when Ernie shoved it through the window at him. I don't want him to get in trouble."

She leaned across the table to peer at me. "Look, from everything you've told me about your grandfather, I think he is just an old man who still believes in his country, his old Germany. We all wanted a new Germany, but not at the cost of this madman, Hitler. Your grandpa can't be blamed for loving his old Germany. But he has to make the choice to separate himself from it now that Hitler is running it, just like my husband did."

I nodded, but still I said nothing.

"I don't think he'll get in trouble if you tell the reporter what you just told me. That he didn't know what was in the pamphlet. But if he does get in trouble, it isn't your fault, Kay. You must show the pamphlet."

I looked into her clear blue eyes, German

eyes. How could she know what was the right thing to do?

She smiled. "You're thinking, *Why should I listen to this lady*," she said then, "*she's German*. Aren't you?"

I blushed. "You're like The Shadow. You can read people's minds."

"No, I can read hearts," she said. "And yours is a good heart, Kay. And I can tell you to do this thing now *because* we are German, my husband and I. And we have made our choices. Do you have anyone fighting in the war?"

"My cousins are fighting," I said. "The sons of my aunt Beth. She's my father's sister."

"Do it for them."

"I don't know my cousins anymore. We never see that family because Amazing Grace won't allow it."

She looked unhappy then. "It's so sad, the way families make war on one another every day," she said, "and make it so hard for children to survive. I'd give anything to have a little girl like you. My husband and I have no children."

She had tears in her eyes. I felt embarrassed.

"Do you know anyone else who's fighting?"

"The only person I knew is dead," I said. And I told her then about my friend Jen's brother.

"Do it for him, then. And do it for your friend Jen."

"She doesn't even speak to me anymore." And I told her about that, too.

"She will," she said. And it sounded like a promise. "She is hurting. She will. Give the pamphlet, Kay. It's the right thing to do. You know that, don't you?"

I said yes, because I did know it. I think I'd known it all along. And just needed someone like her to tell me.

"Come," she said, "I'll drive you home."

CHAPTER
16

I had never been in a car driven by a woman. Amazing Grace doesn't drive. Neither do my sisters.

By the time Mrs. Leudloff dropped me off in front of our long driveway in her old Ford pickup, I thought she was better than The Shadow's Margo, Superman's Lois, and Nick's Nora in *The Thin Man*.

The way she drove, with one elbow resting on the windowsill and one hand guiding the wheel, speaking at the same time, made me feel good. *I'll drive like that someday,* I told myself. *I'll wear red nail polish. I'll know what's right to do in times of crisis. And my hair will always be bobbed and shining, and my lipstick will be handy.*

"Be brave," she said as I slid off the seat, got out, and closed the door.

"I will be. Like Betty Fairfield in *Jack Armstrong*."

She smiled. "Like yourself," she said.

My brothers and Nana were waiting in the kitchen. "Where *were* you?" Martin asked. "The reporter and photographer are here."

"The reporter looks just like Clark Kent!" Tom put in.

"Child," Nana admonished gently as she took the eggs, "what happened to you?"

"I fell and hurt my leg. Mrs. Leudloff drove me home."

"La," Nana said. It's as strong as her language gets. "You'd best go right into the library. Don't bother to change. Hurry!"

I walked through the dim hall and toward the library, feeling to make sure the pamphlet was in my pocket and the pedometer secure on my wrist. My heart was thumping. The boys peered out of the kitchen after me, but Nana wouldn't let them go any farther.

I'll be all right, I told myself. *I've got the magic pedometer. It saved me from Rex, didn't it?*

"Well, this must be the little girl now," the reporter said.

I knew he was the reporter because the other one had the camera.

The reporter was a dead ringer for Clark Kent. He even wore glasses.

"Kay, where *were* you!" Amazing Grace demanded. She was seated in the captain's chair in front of my father's desk. She was wearing her best loose silk dress. Her red hair was all wound in a bun. And I could tell she was doing her best to be like the actress Rita Hayworth. She wore her Tangee lipstick and good silk stockings and best shoes.

"I fell and hurt my leg. Mrs. Leudloff brought me home."

"Tsk, tsk, child. Come in and meet our guests." Amazing Grace looked up at them coyly. "What can I do? It's so hard to keep little girls from being tomboys. She was supposed to be back in time to put on a pretty dress."

"Looks fine as she is," the reporter said. "Just how a little girl should look in the country. Come on in, Kay, and talk to us."

I sat down on the couch.

The reporter took out his notebook, pushed back his hat, and knelt down on one knee in front of me. "Now, do you want to tell us what happened at Ernie's place?"

"I told you that," Amazing Grace purred. "Some men knocked my father over and Kay gave the license-plate number of the car to the police. Wasn't she a bright little girl to do that?"

"Yes, ma'am, she sure was." The reporter nodded at her. "But we'd like to hear it in Kay's own words."

"Kay, tell the nice reporter how Grandpa was knocked down for doing nothing," Amazing Grace said to me.

I looked at her. I saw the warning look in her eyes. I looked at the reporter and photographer. They were waiting patiently. The reporter had kind eyes. But now that I'd heard him speak, his voice was more like Britt Reid's than Clark Kent's. Britt Reid is the Green Hornet. He owns the *Daily Sentinel* and fights all people who try to destroy America.

I thought of Mrs. Leudloff, who drove her Ford pickup with such ease. And ran her egg farm with only a part-time man since her husband went to war.

I thought of Jen's brother, who'd been killed by Hitler's Wolf Pack submarine.

I must do the right thing, I decided. *Like Britt Reid. Or Superman. Or Betty Fairfield. I must fight for truth and justice and go against all people who want to destroy America.*

I have the magic pedometer. It will see me through. I touched it on my wrist.

"It wasn't for nothing," I said.

"What?" Amazing Grace leaned forward in her chair. And she forgot to use the purring tone she'd been using up to now. "Kay, what are you saying?"

"It's true that Grandpa was knocked down for nothing. He didn't deserve to be knocked down by those men. They were picking on him because he has a German accent."

Amazing Grace smiled, settled back in her chair, and preened for the reporter and photographer.

"But he and Ernie were talking about Hitler. And Germany."

"What?" Amazing Grace stood up. "Don't listen to her, gentlemen. She has a very vivid imagination. You know how little girls are."

The reporter was listening. And writing. Fast. And the photographer was snapping my picture while I sat alone on the couch, without Amazing Grace next to me.

"Go on, little girl," the reporter said.

So I went on. "They were talking about the new Germany that Hitler is making. And how the German people are suffering. And about a friend of Ernie's named Hauptmann, who works for the Third Reich. Then Ernie said he had pamphlets sent to him from his friend, and he asked Grandpa to distribute them."

"Enough!" Amazing Grace stood in front of the photographer and tried to push away his camera. "I'm afraid I will have to put a stop to this now. The child is lying."

"Did you see the pamphlets?" the reporter asked.

"I have one. In my pocket."

"Gentlemen," Amazing Grace said, "I'm afraid I'll have to ask you to leave. Can't you see the child is lying? Surely, you're not going to *print* that."

"Ma'am, with all due respect," the reporter said, looking at her fully now, "why don't you let her show us this pamphlet? Then we'll know if she's lying. Can we see it, Kay?"

I stood up and fished it out of my pocket. "I have to say something first," I told him.

"Go ahead," the reporter said.

"Grandpa didn't know what the pamphlet was when Ernie pushed it through the little window at him. And he didn't even have time to read it before he was knocked down."

The reporter nodded. "Fair enough," he

said. And he held out his hand for the pamphlet. I gave it to him.

He read it very fast. Just like Britt Reid would do. Then he looked at Amazing Grace.

"I'd say that the child is doing anything but lying, ma'am," he told her. "Now if you don't mind, in the public interest, I'd like to ask her a couple more questions."

I told them everything. I told them all I knew. And they listened. I told them the whole truth. The way Betty Fairfield would have done. But I didn't forget about justice, either.

"I'm sure Grandpa is a good American," I told him. "He only loves his old country. Lots of German people who live here feel the same way. Mrs. Leudloff, the German lady I go to for eggs, told me that."

"You told Mrs. Leudloff about this?" Amazing Grace was livid.

"Yes." I don't know where I got brave enough to face her, but I did it. "And Mrs. Leudloff said that lots of German-American people are picked on like Grandpa these days."

"You're right, sweetie," the reporter said. And he was still writing, taking down everything I said. "I'm sure the old man was being picked on. And you're a smart little girl to understand that."

Amazing Grace was wringing her hands, and they saw she was upset. So they finished up, thanked her, and took their leave. "The story will be in Sunday's paper," they said.

Then Britt Reid patted me on the shoulder and looked right into my eyes. "You're a brave little girl," he said. "Thank you."

Nobody had ever told me that before. Tears came to my eyes when he said it. And the way he gripped my shoulder made me think that he knew I was in trouble for telling the truth.

"You've got a fine little girl there, ma'am," he said to Amazing Grace. "You and your husband should be proud of her."

I knew he was doing that for me. He winked at me as he walked into the center hall.

"Gentlemen"—Amazing Grace was following them through the hall—"what will happen to my father if you print the story? How will it look for him? And for us?"

The reporter paused at the front door. "It will look like he was doing what the little girl said, asking about his country and how the people there are faring," he said.

"But my father is no Hitler lover," Amazing Grace insisted.

"Nobody said he was, ma'am. This is still America. People have the right to say what they think, read what they wish, and believe in what they want. My guess is, the men who attacked your father will be looked on badly. And Ernie, too."

"Then why print the story?" Amazing Grace asked.

The reporter looked at her with surprise and sadness. "Don't you know, ma'am?"

"No. Quite frankly, I don't," Amazing Grace said.

"Then maybe you ought to ask the little girl. She knows." And he winked at me again as he went out the door.

As soon as they drove out of sight, Amazing Grace turned on me. "So, you're a brave and smart little girl, are you? Well, we'll see how brave you are."

And she looked at Nana and the boys, who were standing in the kitchen doorway, gaping.

"Get the strap behind the kitchen door," she told them.

She kept one of my father's old belts there. And used it on us when she got very angry.

Nobody moved but me.

"No," I said. And I began to run. But she grabbed me by my braids and dragged me through the hall.

"I said get the strap!" she yelled.

"Grace, don't excite yourself," Nana said.

"Don't excite myself? I'm already excited. Thanks to this little demon." And she dragged me by my braids through the kitchen to the back door.

"No!" Martin ran to her. "Don't hit her. She did what was right."

She hit Martin in the face. Then she grabbed the strap and started hitting me with it with one hand while she held me by my braids with the other.

"There, and there, and there," she said, swinging the strap. "Now we'll see how brave and smart you are."

"No, no!" Martin was yelling. And he tried to grab the strap from her. A few times he got hit for his trouble.

Tom was crying, "Stop it, stop it!" She'd hit him enough times with the strap for him to know how it felt.

It felt bad. It felt like someone was burning me with hot irons, on my back and shoulders and legs. I screamed. I thrashed. "No, no, stop!" I cried.

But she didn't stop.

It was Nana who finally stopped her. "Grace. Stop it! Now!"

Nana stepped into the fray. She even got caught once with the strap herself. "Grace, stop it. This is not how I raised you. What's the matter with you? Grace, you'll hurt yourself. You'll hurt the baby."

That stopped her. She let me go. And I ran. I ran out the back door, across the driveway and lawns, through the fields, and down to the brook. I ran, crying and hurting and sore.

I ran, and I was not brave.

I'd known she would be mad. And I'd promised myself to be brave. Like Hop Harrigan is behind enemy lines. Like Betty Fairfield when she went with Jack Armstrong and her father, chopping their way through the Philippine jungles. Like Superman, standing up for truth, justice, and the American way, and like Britt Reid, who fights all people who try to destroy America.

But when my time came to be brave, I was just a screaming little girl, begging Amazing Grace to stop, and running scared through the fields.

She'd ruined it all, all the good I tried to do to keep America safe. The good feeling

I'd had about doing right was gone. She'd killed it. The reporter had been wrong. I wasn't smart and brave. I was dirty and hurting and ashamed.

And worst of all, the magic pedometer hadn't saved me.

CHAPTER

17

I stayed down by the brook all afternoon. I took off my blouse and washed myself by dipping it into the clear water. My legs and shoulders and back hurt so. The whole world hurt.

It was full of treachery, evil, and betrayal. I'd tried to do right and fight for truth and justice, and it didn't work.

On all our radio programs, doing what's right works for the heroes and heroines. They always win their battles against evil.

I'd lost. It was probably my fault somehow, I was sure of it. I'd done something wrong. I'd missed some clue that I probably would go on missing forever. I was useless.

I hung my blouse on a tree limb to dry. Then, because it hadn't been any good to me anyway, I took off the magic pedometer and set it down on a rock, and sat down to think.

I would never go back to the house. I decided that while I was still crying. I would live down here by the brook. I'd get Martin and Tom to bring me sandwiches and water and a blanket. If I went back, Amazing Grace would make life more miserable for me than it already was.

By the time I stopped crying, I decided that wasn't a good plan. It was a better idea to run away.

Amazing Grace had run away once. She'd had a fight with my father, and I'd stood in her bedroom watching her put on her Coty powder and her Tangee lipstick, and patting her hair and looking at herself in the large oval mirror of her dressing table.

"I'm running away," she'd said.

"Can I go with you?"

She said yes and so we walked all the way up our road, the River Road, to Route 6. Then we started walking north. I was very excited about the idea of running away. I didn't worry about where we would live or how. It was the idea of running away that was the important thing.

More important, Amazing Grace had taken me with her!

But then, before we'd walked too far, my father came by in the car and asked her to come home. Amazing Grace got into the car and made me get in, too.

I was so disappointed in her. She hadn't really wanted to run away. All she wanted was for my father to come after her. But then something else disappointed me more. "I don't mind that you ran away," my father said to her, "but did you have to take Kay?"

"Yes," she answered. "To make you worry more."

It was then that I realized that Amazing Grace hadn't taken me with her because she wanted me. But because she wanted to hurt my father.

I was thinking I'd do the same thing, just walk up River Road and head north on Route 6, when I saw Martin walking through the fields toward me. I got up and put on my blouse. Because Sister Brigitta said a girl should always be modest.

"Nana said you should come home," Martin said. He'd brought water and bread with peanut butter on it.

"I'm not ever coming home again. I'm going to run away."

"Where?"

"I don't know. It doesn't matter. I'm sure nobody would care or come after me."

"Me and Tom would care. You can't do that."

"Why?"

He thought for a moment. "Because you wouldn't be able to listen to *Hop Harrigan* again. He and Tank Tinker are still in that Japanese prison camp. And the Nazis are going to try to kill Superman with kryptonite tonight."

"I don't care about all that anymore," I told him.

His eyes went wide. "You don't care about our radio programs?"

"No. They're all phony."

Martin was unbelieving. "How can you say that?"

"I can. All those people like Superman and Hop Harrigan and Jack Armstrong are only stories. They tell us to be brave and tell the truth and fight evil and keep on punching. Well, it didn't work this afternoon for me. I tried to do the right thing and look what happened."

Martin did the only thing he knew how to do when things got too much for him. He took out a cigarette, lighted it, and began to smoke. I ate my peanut-butter bread and drank my water.

"Nana says you did the right thing," he said finally.

My ears perked up. "Nana? I thought she'd be mad at me."

"No. She says she told Grandpa to stay away from that place. And to stop talking about the old Germany. She says there is no more Germany and, *la,* Grandpa is a fool sometimes. And maybe now he'll learn his lesson."

Tears came to my eyes. Nana. She'd stand by me. I had a brief feeling of hope. Nana was a good person to have around. Like Tonto on *The Lone Ranger.*

No, I must stop thinking about my radio programs. All they'd done was get me into trouble.

"What's my pedometer doing on that rock?" Martin asked.

I picked it up and handed it to him. "You can have it back. It doesn't work. If it did, it would have protected me from Amazing Grace. I don't believe in it anymore. Take it."

Martin regarded it solemnly. "You have to believe in it for it to work," he said.

"Well, I don't anymore, so take it." Then

I had another thought. "Daddy will kill me when he comes home. I upset Amazing Grace," I said.

"No, he doesn't want trouble. You know how he hates trouble. And Nana says she'll talk to him."

"But he lets Amazing Grace get away with everything. Why does he do that?"

"He has to," Martin said.

"Why?"

"He has to keep peace."

"Well, I'm still not coming home. Daddy won't care. The only one he cares about is Amazing Grace."

Martin looked at me with his brown, steady gaze. "I'm going to tell you something now, to prove you're wrong," he said. "If you believe me, you must promise to come home. But even if you don't believe me, you have to promise never to let anybody know I told you. Okay?"

I promised.

"You know how he takes us to Coney Island whenever we go to Nana's on a Saturday? And how you always cry because he won't take you?"

"Yes."

"Well, we don't go to Coney Island."

I felt something coming. Something big and powerful, like a locomotive, rushing right at me. "Where do you go?"

"On a secret mission," Martin said.

I believed him. He wasn't lying. The look on his face told me he wasn't. He was about to tell me something that would explain everything and make things all right again. "What kind of secret mission?"

"We go and visit Mother's grave."

The world got softer all of a sudden. The hard edges softened, the sense of evil lifted, and I felt hope instead of betrayal.

"You go to Mother's grave?" I whispered.

"Yes. She's buried in Brooklyn. Daddy puts flowers on it. He gives us each one and we put them on it, too."

I was silent for a long time. So was Martin. He finished his cigarette and threw it into the brook. "So now will you come home?"

I said yes. And I went home, walking back across the fields to that house where Amazing Grace held sway over us all, like some kind of evil goddess.

Or thought she did. But now I knew she didn't. Because she didn't have all of my father's loyalty. I knew that now.

In a corner of his heart, he still loved my

mother. As long as I knew that, I could go on.

At the end of the field, Martin turned to me and held out the pedometer. "You keep it," he said, "it's yours."

I knew how much it meant to him. "No, I don't want it. I told you, it's no good to me."

"The magic isn't in the pedometer," he said. "All it does is bring out the good things in the person who wears it."

"Like what?"

"Courage and good luck and faith."

"I don't have any of those things."

"Yes, you do," he said. "Just keep it. Some people don't know they have these things. After a while, when you know, you can give it back to me."

I hesitated.

"Maybe it's worked for you already," he said, "and you just don't know it."

I thought of Rex that morning. And how he could have killed me and didn't. Had it worked for me already?

I grinned. "All right," I said. And I took it.

When my father got home that night, Amazing Grace had taken to her bed. He came down from their room, grim faced.

"The child wasn't to blame," Nana told him in the kitchen.

He looked at me. Then he looked at Martin and Tom. "Just be very quiet, all of you, the next few days. Kay, you'd better stay out of her way."

"I'll keep Kay busy," Nana said.

He was happy with that. We had supper and he said no more about it.

CHAPTER
18

Sunday came, the last day of our Easter vacation, the day the story about me was to be in the newspaper.

Early in the morning I heard a noise.

Amazing Grace was yelling.

"John, oh, John," she was saying, "do something!"

Their voices came from downstairs.

I sat up in bed. Had I been dreaming? I looked across the room. Elizabeth's and Mary's beds were empty. I heard men's voices downstairs. I got up, put on my robe, and crept out into the hallway.

Strange men were in the house. They were carrying Amazing Grace through the hall on a stretcher.

"John!" she was wailing.

Mary, Elizabeth, Martin, and Tom were downstairs. Mary was crying. Elizabeth stood next to her. They were both in robes and slippers.

"It will be all right, children," Nana was saying. "Come into the kitchen."

They followed her into the kitchen. "It's too early," Mary was saying. "It's too early."

They took Amazing Grace away in the ambulance. I thought Mary was saying it was too early in the morning. I didn't understand until that night what she was really talking about.

The story about me was in the Sunday *Waterville Times,* but nobody even bothered to read it. I sneaked a look at it when everyone else was busy.

The reporter wrote that I was "a sadlooking little girl who looked like Margaret O'Brien and had the courage to come out and speak about what she thought was wrong, even though it involved a member of her family."

Courage! He said I had courage! Was it like Martin said, then? That sometimes you didn't know you had it?

I read further. The reporter had written

that I spoke up about the pamphlet for my friend's brother, who'd gone down when his ship was torpedoed. I'd forgotten that I'd told him that.

The rest of it was about German Americans in this country, how they are persecuted and how Ernie's place would probably lose its liquor license. And Ernie had been taken in for questioning for giving out the pamphlets.

It said the hecklers had been arrested. But that Grandpa was innocent of all wrongdoing. He was only an old man concerned about his old country, it said. Not a Nazi sympathizer. Nazi sympathizers had been convicted before in our state, and the New Jersey Supreme Court had overturned their conviction because it violated the New Jersey Constitution.

I didn't understand it all. But I breathed a sigh of relief that Grandpa wouldn't be arrested. And my picture was there, too. There I was, in my dungarees, blouse, and braids.

Margaret O'Brien? Yes, I supposed so. That's who I was like. Not Shirley Temple in her fluffy dresses, singing and tap-dancing her way through life.

Margaret O'Brien has tragedy in all her movies. Look at the way she buried all her dolls in *Meet Me in St. Louis.*

How about that, I told myself. *Wait until the kids in school see this.* How about that.

The Shadow was going against a demented hypnotist who wanted to take over the army when my father came home from the hospital that night.

John Barclay, the announcer, was telling us how the weed of crime bears bitter fruit. My father came into the dining room, where we were all huddled around the old Philco radio.

"And so, John," Nana said, "tell us, what's happened?"

"Your daughter's had a baby girl," he told her.

Mary jumped up and down. "A baby sister. We've got a baby sister," she said.

Martin and Tom tried to look happy. So did Elizabeth. I said nothing. *I won't be the baby in the family anymore,* I thought. *Maybe now I can be a big sister. Maybe now somebody will look up to me.*

"I've kept your dinner, John," Nana said.

He went into the kitchen with her.

"And how is Grace?" I heard Nana asking.

"Weak, but resting. It was hard on her, Nana."

"It's always hard on women."

"The baby had to be put in an incubator," he told her. "It's only four pounds. We don't know if it's going to make it."

In the dining room my brothers and sisters and I looked at each other. "What's an incubator?" I asked.

"It's something they put a premature baby in to keep it alive," Elizabeth said.

"What's premature?" I asked again.

Nobody spoke for a moment. Then Elizabeth spoke again. "It's when a baby comes before its time. And is too small."

The Baby Snooks Show was coming on next, sponsored by Post cereal. Her daddy and mommy are always fighting about something. And her daddy is very burdened by her mommy. Like mine. Baby Snooks is always getting him into trouble.

"*Whyyy, Daddy?*" she keeps asking to drive him crazy. It's a comedy.

"This baby came six weeks early," Mary was saying.

Whyyy, Mary? I wanted to ask. *Whyyy?* But I didn't. Because I knew.

The others knew, too.

It was on account of me. Because I'd gotten Amazing Grace upset. Because I'd told the reporters the truth about her father.

We sat listening to *Baby Snooks*. Nobody talked any more about our baby.

CHAPTER

19

Every summer the girls of the Golden Band have their pictures in the social section of the newspaper. The photographer shoots them posed on the beach, on vacation. Together, always together.

Now I had my picture in the newspaper, with a story. What would they have to say about it? Would they see I wasn't so unworthy, after all?

But on Monday morning in school, all I got was mean remarks about being Margaret O'Brien.

"A kid actress!" Cathy Doyle said.

"You could have at least rolled up your dungarees," Amy Crynan scolded.

They have a song they sing:

"We are St. Bridget's girls,
we wear our hair in curls,
we wear our dungarees
rolled up right to our knees."

My dungarees hadn't been rolled up properly.

"God, I'd die if they put in the paper that I went for ice cream with my *grandfather*," Rosemary Winter mumbled.

It is not the thing to do, to be seen socializing with your grandfather. If you go for ice cream with anybody, it should be a friend your own age.

"You did it for Jen's brother?" Eileen Keifer asked. "Don't you think she feels bad enough? We're trying to help her forget!"

Jen didn't look at me.

I'd done everything wrong. I couldn't do anything right in the eyes of the Golden Band. I was glad I hadn't been trying.

But I couldn't forget about Jen. It was like someone was kicking me in the stomach every time I saw her disappear around a corner with the girls of the Golden Band, all of them joking and singing, giggling and carrying on. Jen never joked or giggled or carried on like that. What were they doing to her?

Our house was very quiet. All that could be heard was the grandfather clock ticking in the hall and Mary's sobbing. The radio was off, even though it was Sunday night, when all the best programs are on.

But even though it was off, I could hear its sounds. I could hear the announcer of *Lights Out* telling us it was the witching hour, when dogs howl and evil is let loose on the world.

I could hear the lonely police siren from *Gang Busters*, wailing in the night.

I could hear The Shadow's cackling laugh.

I sat on the stairs and put my hands over my ears. Still, I could hear Walter Winchell opening his news show, tapping his telegraph keys and telling Mr. and Mrs. North and South America, all ships at sea, and the *whole world,* that as he went to press he'd gotten news that Mr. and Mrs. John Hennings's baby girl had died last night in Waterville's hospital.

I could hear Baby Snooks's sad and whiny voice, saying, *"Whyyy,* Daddy, *whyyy?"*

My father was in their bedroom with Amazing Grace, who was very quiet. I don't know where my brothers were. Outside, I suppose. It was better outside. Elizabeth was doing the supper dishes. The radio sounds kept going round and round in my head as I sat there. And through it all, I could hear Mary in her room, sobbing.

Then, all of a sudden, something almost magical happened. Somebody downstairs, maybe Elizabeth, had the radio on, real low. And there was Vera Lynn, singing her song about how we should keep smiling through.

I couldn't believe it! It was just what Queenie told me to do when things get bad. I listened, tears coming to my eyes, as Vera Lynn's husky voice sang about how we would all meet again and until then we had to keep smiling through.

And for a minute I felt Queenie there beside me.

"Oh, Queenie," I whispered, "how I miss you! But it's just like you're right here when she sings that song. I'll try, Queenie, I'll try!"

The song even drowned out the sound of Mary's sobbing.

We went on. We went to school every day. Mary and Elizabeth and my father went to work. Nana cooked and kept order.

Nobody said anything to me. Nobody blamed me. But I blamed myself. A hundred times in the next week I wished I hadn't told the truth to that reporter and gotten Amazing Grace so upset that she'd had her baby too early.

As for the newspaper story about me, nobody in my house even mentioned it. Only Mrs. Leudloff smiled and patted me on the head and told me how proud she was of me, when I went for eggs.

And when I'd told her, on my last visit, that the baby was sickly, she said, "I lost my only child. What God decides will be, will be."

I couldn't tell her that I, not God, was to blame. She'd just smile and pat me on the head and say, *Have another caramel, you're far too serious for a little girl.* I didn't want her to know I'd caused the baby's death. She believed in me.

Amazing Grace sat in the rocker in the dining room in front of the floor-to-ceiling windows. It was Sunday.

She was just sitting and brooding. She'd been sitting there like that for a week, since the baby died. She hardly ate when Nana brought her food to her. She didn't speak to us. And she didn't cry at all.

Everyone was worried about her.

"If she doesn't snap out of it soon," Mary had said this morning, "she may go into depression."

"She isn't even mean anymore," Tom said.

My brothers and I were sitting out in the barn on stacks of hay, talking about it.

"What's depression?" I asked Martin.

"It means when you can't stop being sad."

Oh. It sounded like just the opposite of smiling through. But then, Amazing Grace had never been the kind to smile too much in the first place. We all knew that.

"If she gets any more depressed, we're all in for it," Martin said. "Daddy's very worried. He says we all have to be nice to her."

"Maybe I can do something nice," I said.

"The nicest thing you could do is leave her alone," Martin told me.

Tom agreed. "What could *you* do?" he hooted. "She doesn't like you, Kay. It's Mary she likes. She hates you almost as much as she hates Elizabeth."

But I had an idea. I knew, too, that if Amazing Grace got any more crazy than she already was, we'd all be in trouble. But I had another reason for wanting to try with her.

I felt sorry for her. I didn't think anything could make her sit there in that chair like that, folded up like a dying flower. *It must be terrible, losing a baby,* I thought.

Why, I would feel terrible losing Mary Frances.

I said nothing to my brothers. They wouldn't understand.

Later on, after Sunday dinner, when my father was napping, my brothers were at the brook playing, Mary and Elizabeth were at the movies, and Nana was sewing, I went to the room I shared with my sisters and opened the closet.

There, where my few clothes hung, I took the feed-bag dress off its hanger.

Amazing Grace had finished it right before she had the baby. I hadn't worn it yet. I'd said I didn't want to. Then everything happened so fast, with the baby coming, that nobody cared.

I took off my dungarees and blouse and slipped the feed-bag dress over my head. Then I went to look in the mirror. It was full length. I looked at myself in the dress.

I looked terrible. I looked worse than Margaret O'Brien in *Journey for Margaret,* when she played a war orphan.

Perfect, I decided. And I slipped quietly downstairs.

Amazing Grace was still in the rocker in the dining room. I walked up to her and stood on the small braided rug in front of her.

"I'm wearing the dress you made," I said.

She didn't seem to hear me at first. Then her eyes went over the dress, which was sort of a tan color with small flowers on it. She nodded slowly. "It looks good."

"Yes," I said. "I'd wear it to school, except that I have to wear my uniform."

"The last week of school they let you wear regular clothes. You can wear it then."

Oh God, I prayed, *how can I do that?* "Yes," I agreed. "Wait until the other girls see it. They'll all be jealous."

She started to rock back and forth. "My baby girl is dead," she said.

"I know. I'm sorry."

"So small. She was so small. And so perfect. She was a perfect little girl. And she had blond hair and blue eyes."

I took a deep breath. My hair is dark, my eyes brown. She always said I was too dark. I knew she liked blond-haired, blue-eyed little girls. *She would love the girls in the Golden Band*, I thought.

"I wish I could have seen her," I said.

"Her name was Louise."

I felt a stab of envy. Louise. Such a fine name. Not a plain, old-fashioned name like Kay. You could do wonderful things with a name like Louise.

Amazing Grace started to cry then. And for a moment I got scared. *I'd made her cry.*

She cried in great, heaving sobs. "All I ever wanted was a little girl," she blubbered. "My own little girl. That's all I ever wanted."

I didn't know what to do. I got scared. I wanted to reach out and hug her, but I didn't dare. My throat went dry and I felt a great bursting sadness inside me, like I was going to drown.

"Why can't I be your little girl?" I asked softly.

She stopped crying and looked at me for a moment. I stood straight, in my feed-bag dress, with my brown eyes and brown hair. And I knew what she was thinking. That her little girl would look like Shirley Temple, all round pinkness and dimples with blond shining curls. Not like Margaret O'Brien. Or like me, with dark, straight hair, skinny, with a sad face.

And I knew something else then, too. *Her little girl would never wear a feed-bag dress.* And she would wear Mary Janes, all the time.

Then she started crying again. It sounded awful. "All I ever wanted was a little girl," she wailed.

Nana came rushing into the room. I heard my father come running down the stairs.

"What is it?" Nana asked. "What have you done to her, Kay?"

I stepped back, frightened.

My father looked sternly at me. "What did you do?"

"I wanted to make her smile," I said tearfully.

"Good, Grace, good," Nana was saying. "Cry, child, cry."

Amazing Grace kept right at it.

"It's good, John," Nana said, turning to him. "The doctor said she must cry. And she hasn't until now. Whatever Kay said to her, it helped. She'll be all right now, John. She's crying."

My father pushed me out of the way and went to put his arms around Amazing Grace. He held her.

I didn't understand. I'd tried to make Amazing Grace happy again. I thought you had to keep smiling through, not cry.

I ran from the room. If what I did was good, why didn't they thank me?

My father hadn't looked at me at all.

CHAPTER
20

I was very frightened. I don't remember ever being so scared because of the war. We were having another air raid in school, only this time, instead of our diving under the desks, the nuns had ushered us into the great arching center hall.

It's lined on both sides with metal lockers. On either end of the hall, huge staircases with fat, cherry banisters reach to the upper level.

Everyone was talking in a buzzing whisper, wondering what was going on. Sister Mary Louise shushed us, severely. She stood in the middle of the hall.

"Be quiet! We will now pray until the sirens stop."

So we prayed. And the lonely, soulsearing sirens howled over us and echoed through the silent building. I thought they would never stop.

I waited for the bombs to fall. I always thought bombs were going to fall during air raids, that the Nazis or Japs had broken through our coastal defenses and were going to drop bombs on us like the Nazis did on London.

Then I saw Jen a few paces ahead of me in line.

She was looking at me.

She hadn't looked at me all spring in school. And it was now the first week in June. School would let out on the fifteenth; today was the sixth.

At home, things had pretty much quieted down. We weren't exactly smiling through, but we were getting on. Amazing Grace was getting better. Nana was still with us and would stay until the summer, if necessary. Then she had to go home. Grandpa ate his meals in the restaurant where he worked, so he was okay for a while. But we all knew that sooner or later Nana had to go.

My father was looking for a new house-keeper.

Who would she be? Who could we stand? Who could stand us?

For a moment I met Jen's eyes. And I saw

something in them. What? Was she sorry? Did she remember all the good times we'd had? What?

I couldn't think with those sirens blaring. And then they stopped. The hall was strangely silent. We all sighed in relief. But Sister Mary Louise held up her hand and spoke.

"Boys and girls, today is a very special day. And this is why I have assembled you in this hall instead of having the usual air-raid drill."

Everyone waited.

"Today something very important is happening with our soldiers. They are fighting a terrible battle. And we must pray for them."

So we prayed again. And we sang the song we usually sang to the Blessed Virgin, asking her to help our valiant soldiers.

Then it was lunchtime.

I walked with my head down as my classmates rushed forward toward the lunchroom. I ate alone now. Oh, it was in the same lunchroom, sometimes at the same table, but I sat a little away from them and listened to what went on.

All spring Jen had sat in the middle of the

Golden Band. And laughed and told jokes and repeated gossip.

Well, I thought, *at least she's smiling through.*

Sometimes I didn't go to the cafeteria. Now that the weather was nice, I'd take my lunch outside to the shady part of the schoolyard and sit under a tree. It was better than having to sit and see my best friend with the Golden Band.

"Kay?"

I turned. Jen was standing there. I waited.

"I wanted to talk to you."

I felt a lot of things at once. A rush of joy, surprise, and anger. "Why?"

"I have to tell you something."

"What's wrong? Did the Golden Band get sick of you? You're not popular anymore?"

I was mad. And I saw no reason why I had to be nice after the way she'd hurt me so. I always knew they'd get tired of her sooner or later. After all, she still ate cream-cheese sandwiches and wore brown oxfords.

"Please, Kay, there's something I have to tell you."

"I don't want to hear it." We were at the corner in the hall where you turned left to go to the cafeteria or right to go outside.

I turned right.

She followed me. "I'll come with you," she said.

I walked out into the warm sunshine and shrugged. "It's a free country." I felt very grown-up, saying it. Martin said it all the time.

I walked across the paved schoolyard to the little patch of green. She was still following me. I sat under a tree and opened my lunch box and took out my tomato sandwich.

"Kay, will you listen to me?"

"Why should I?"

"Because it's something important that you should know."

"What could you tell me that I should know?"

"How your baby sister really died."

The sun was very hot, suddenly. I felt it spiraling down out of the sky, right at me. There was a droning in my ears, too. *Must be a mosquito.*

"What are you saying?"

"My mother knows. She said I should tell you."

Of course! Her mother worked on the new-baby floor of the hospital! I could hardly breathe. Was it possible her mother knew something?

It was. I saw the look in Jen's eyes.

"Tell me," I said.

"First, you have to know that my mother wants me to tell you because she read the story in the paper where you told about the pamphlet and your grandfather. My mother said you must have gotten into big trouble over that."

I shrugged.

"She said, 'That little girl is carrying a heavy burden. And her stepmother had the baby right after. I saw her in the hospital. She was yelling something about her father not loving Germany or Hitler when they brought her in.' "

I nodded. My mouth went dry.

"Then she said you must be blaming yourself because the baby came early. She heard the doctor say that Grace is a person full of anger and that he'd told her she had to calm down about a lot of things. Or the baby would be premature."

"What have you got to tell me, Jen?"

"Mom said that if you tell anybody, she could lose her job. So you've got to promise not to tell."

I nodded yes.

"Especially not at home. Not anybody."

"Okay, okay, I promise."

"Okay. The baby died because they took her out of the incubator."

I just stared at her. "I don't understand."

"She needed the incubator to stay alive. But there aren't enough incubators to go around."

"Why?"

"Because of the war. They took her out to give it to another baby. The doctors decided to do that. They had to decide to do that. They had to decide which baby to give it to. Another baby needed it more."

I swallowed. There was a great roaring sound in my ears.

"She didn't die because she was born too soon, Kay." Jen gave great emphasis to every word as she said them. "Oh, sure, she would have lived if she hadn't been born so soon. But two things you have to keep in mind here."

And she enumerated them on her fingers.

"First, the doctor warned your stepmother to stay calm. Anything could have made her have that baby early. From what you've told me, she's always upset about something."

I nodded. "Yes, but this time I did it."

"Maybe next time it would have been something else. Or somebody else. And second, even though the baby was born early, it *would have lived* if they didn't take it out of the incubator. My mother wanted you to know this. Only, you can't tell anybody."

I just sat there taking it all in. From somewhere way behind me I heard the school bell ring. Lunch hour was over.

"The war killed the baby, Kay," Jen said softly. "Just like the war killed my brother. My mother said that when the war is over, there will be enough incubators for all babies. And even if they're born too early, they'll live."

I felt a shuddering inside me. At the same time I felt light, as if somebody had lifted an old, soggy, wet coat off my shoulders.

"It's okay if you want to cry, Kay," she said. "My mother says people have to cry. She says people have to do something to get over their grief . . . I know I've treated you rotten."

"It's okay," I said.

"No, it isn't. But when my brother was killed, I didn't know what to do. Then, all of a sudden, the Golden Band was there, showing me. We fooled around a lot and laughed and joked. I acted crazy, like I didn't care about anything."

"You smiled through," I told her.

"What?"

"Like in the Vera Lynn song, you kept smiling through."

"Yeah." She shook her head. "Whatever you want to call it, that's what I did, I guess."

"Did it help?" I asked.

"It made me feel better while I was doing it. Mom says everybody acts different trying to get over grief. Mom worked longer hours when my brother died. That helped her."

"Amazing Grace just sat in a rocker and wouldn't talk to anybody," I told her.

She nodded. We sat in silence for a moment. "Do you feel better about the baby now?" she asked. "I have to tell my mom. She's worried about you."

"I feel better, yeah," I said. "Tell your mom thanks. But I guess I'll always feel, a little bit, that it was my fault."

"My mom wasn't on duty yet when it happened," she explained. "When she came on, another nurse told her. Mom wouldn't have let it happen if she'd been there, Kay."

I sniffed. "I know."

"We've both lost somebody to the war now," she said.

I looked at her. "There's something different about you," I said.

"I got rid of my bangs."

"No, it's more than that."

"What?"

"I don't know. You're not a kid anymore."

She shrugged. "I guess I had to grow up, some."

"You're different. Not like my old friend Jen anymore."

She looked down at the grass. She ran her finger through it. "I could be your new friend Jen," she said. "If you wanted."

For one long moment, I couldn't speak, for the lump in my throat. Then I reached out to her. At the same time she reached for me.

"I want it," I said.

We walked back to the school together. "My mom says this is D-Day," she told me.

"What's that?"

"I don't know. But Mom was real happy when I left for school. She said if our soldiers do good today, the war could soon be over."

"Wow!" I said. "No more air raids, no more rationing, no more scrap drives."

"No more boys killed," she said. And I decided I'd been right. She was not a kid anymore. And I had some catching up to do to keep up with her.

CHAPTER
21

D-Day didn't end the war, though it was a great victory in Europe. All we had to do now was beat the Japs.

A few days after Jen and I made up, it came to me what I had to do to catch up with her.

After all, I *needed* to catch up with her. We were going into sixth grade together in the fall.

Sixth-graders aren't kids anymore. In public school they're considered old enough to be in junior high.

Already, in our school, when we walked down the street from St. Bridget's School to St. Bridget's Church, the girls of the Golden Band were screaming and carrying on when the boys took their hats.

Before now they had ignored the boys. Before now the boys hadn't bothered taking their hats.

Life was changing. I had to be just as grown-up and ready as all the others for whatever was coming next.

To be honest, Martin is the one who led me to what I had to do, although he didn't know it.

He was doing another scrap drive. He does one every couple of weeks, tugging his old red wagon around to all the neighbors, begging for discarded tires, metal, cans, anything that will help bring us closer to victory.

"Rubber is the hardest thing to get anymore," he told me that morning. "All the old tires are gone. Know where there's any old rubber around, Kay?"

"How would I know?"

He grinned. "Want to give your rubber baby doll this time?"

It was the same way he'd asked for Mary Frances a dozen times, before he started down the drive with the red wagon.

Always I said no.

He was used to it.

This time I didn't say no. This time I didn't say anything for a minute.

Then I sighed while the enormity of the thought washed over me.

Yes, I knew what I had to do. "Wait, Martin," I said. "Wait."

So he waited. And I went into the house and upstairs into my sisters' room.

Mary Frances was sitting there in the middle of my bed, like she always sat, with her little arms outstretched, waiting for me. She was wearing her new dress that Nana had made.

I remembered how I'd told Martin that I could never give her to the scrap drive because they'd tear her apart. And she'd die.

And you can't die when you've just had a new dress made for you.

I know different now. Dolls don't die. Babies do.

And you *can* die even if you have a new dress.

Nana had made a lovely new dress for Amazing Grace's baby. The baby had died anyway. The dress was packed away now, in tissue paper.

Dolls aren't babies. They're toys.

I know that now. Even though I still don't

know, and maybe never will know, why when you're good and do the right thing, sometimes it all goes bad for you.

I picked up Mary Frances and held her against me. Tears blurred my eyes and I felt a great bursting of sadness in me again, like I was drowning. A little part of me didn't want to let go of her. But I had to.

"I'll always love you, Mary Frances," I said. "But you have to go to war now. To save our boys who are fighting for us. So maybe some other girl like Jen doesn't lose her brother."

She understood, if dolls can understand. I know she did. She just kept smiling, smiling right through.

So I brought her downstairs and outside. "Here," I said. And I thrust Mary Frances at him.

Martin's eyes went wide. "Are you sure?" he asked.

"Yes, I'm sure."

"She's your only doll. And dolls are hard to get. You probably won't be able to get another one until the war is over."

"She's only a piece of rubber," I said. "And by the time the war is over, I'll be too grown-up to play with dolls. I'm too grown-up now. Take her!"

He took her.

"And you might as well take this, too. I don't need it anymore." I undid the pedometer from my wrist and held it out to him.

Martin grinned. "Guess you don't," he said. And he took it.

I turned and ran into the house so he wouldn't see me bawling.

In August, for my birthday, I received a package from New York.

It was from Queenie.

It was a pair of blue hand-knitted mittens. And a note.

"Doing fine," she wrote. "My prince will soon be my husband. I'm working in a war plant now, like Rosie the Riveter. We're both saving money. Sometimes I'm so tired, I don't know my own name.

"Saw the story about you in the paper. Mrs. Leudloff sent it to me. I'm so proud of you, Kay! I told you that you'd do something wonderful someday, didn't I? Only that's just the start.

"No more Shirley Temple, I see. Margaret O'Brien now, is it? Yes, I can see the resemblance. That's okay for now, but that'll pass, too. Someday you'll do more fine things and be happy being just Kay.

"Keep smiling through and we'll meet again someday, maybe when the war is over. Love, Queenie."

There was no return address. But I'm hoping. Just like everybody else is hoping they'll meet again with the people who mean most to them, when the war is over.

BIBLIOGRAPHY

Mappen, Marc, *Jerseyana, The Underside of New Jersey History*, 1992, New Brunswick, N.J., Rutgers University Press

Sulzberger, C.L. *The American Heritage Picture History of World War II*, 1966, New York, N.Y., American Heritage/Bonanza Books

The Ladies Home Journal, October, 1942, The Curtis Publishing Company, Independence Square, Philadelphia, PA

Dunning, John. *Tune in Yesterday, The Ultimate Encyclopedia of Old-time Radio, 1925–1976*, 1976. Englewood Cliffs, N.J., Prentice Hall